SHE

GLOBAL VISION PRESS

World Class Writings for Global Citizens

Global Vision Press, entered the book-publishing arena with the view, ideal and vision of '*vasudhaiva kutumbakam*'—may the whole world be one family, an ancient Indian adage. Holding on to this vision, we propose to attract as well as involve every enlightened human being in the designing and developing of the globalized life and culture of our world—by way of the WORDS.

Our special invite to writers, of this new global world, who triumph over their creativity and are willing to dissolve boundaries, to bring literature closer to global citizens.

Introducing some of the finest world class writings

1. **REALITY REPAIR** by **William Cottringer** **(Self Help)**
   (*Fixing a Lot by Knowing a Little)*
2. **TURN YOUR LIFE AROUND WITH REIKI**
   (*The Complete Guide to the Science and Practice of Reiki)*
   by **Anil Bhatnagar** **(Self Help)**
3. **SHAKE UP INDIA** by **Jayant V. Narlikar** **(Inspire)**
   (*The Need of the Times)*
4. **THE CHANGE MAKER** by **Subhash Agrawal** **(Inspire)**
   (*A Crusade Through Letters)*
5. **TIGER TANTRA** by **Ganga Prasad Vimal** **(Fiction)**
   (*English version of an unusual and highly acclaimed Hindi novel 'Mrigaantak')*
6. **SHE** by **Dixy Gandhi** **(Fiction)**
   (*Stories of Modern Indian Women)*
7. **A CODER'S COCKTAIL!** by **Shashwat Rai** **(Fiction)**
   (*What not to do in IT...)*
8. **THE KINDLING TOUCH** by **Debabrata Dasgupta** **(Biographies)**
   (*Biography of Madame Curie)*
9. **THE LUCK OF THE JEWS** by **Michael Benanav** **(True Story)**
   (*A True Story of Love, Death and Survival in the Holocaust)*
10. **THANK YOU, IDI AMIN** by **Mohezin Tejani** **(True Story)**
    (*A Memoir of the Asian Exodus)*

SHE

(Stories of Modern Indian Women)

Dixy Gandhi

GLOBAL VISION PRESS

Published by Global Vision Press

ISBN 978-93-80707-22-8 (Flexi Back)

GLOBAL VISION PRESS
4855/24, Ansari Road, Daryaganj
New Delhi-110002, India

This is a work of fiction. Names, characters, places and incidents are either the product of author's imagination or are used fictitiously and any resemblance to any actual person, living or dead, events or locales is entirely coincidental.

Typeset in Baskerville by
AJAY ARTS
New Delhi

Printed at
STAR PRINT-O-BIND
New Delhi

Dedicated to *'My Mother'*

for her endless support to my every endeavor

and

my niece *'Gabbu'*,

for I stole time from her to write...

Preface

"Picasso would not be Picasso; if he had stopped painting just like that... you've to find yourself."

These words were said to me when I stopped writing just like that. The reasons for stopping were plenty, the rat race of life, an effort to fit into the corporate world, the concerns of everyday life when money, luxuries and career become everything.

But the reason for writing again was just one—the love of writing. I needed a little nudge and those words provided it. I was back to my first love and then everything else became secondary.

"You have the power to kill, in the knife you hold
But for centuries my story will be told."

Miya added with melancholy.

"A weapon you not need to be able to kill.
Just a fair knowledge of Achilles' Heel"

Chhaya says with a composed smile.

What started as an effort to understand the depths of human nature, conversations which I believe every independent, urban youth of today have, ended in a collection of twelve short stories.

All the events mentioned in the stories never happened, but the central theme is omnipresent. The first story of the collection revolves around me. I am somehow the girl who walked the by lanes of Shimla, lost in thought, questioning my sanity and trying to find answers to things that have troubled me since long.

The rationalization, the methodical thinking with which every person who is in the age group of 20–30 was brought up has made us cynical to some extent, but we are also the same people who believe in reincarnations, ghosts and our dreams. We are the amalgamation of tradition and science, something which I believe is on the verge of extinction. The teens of today are too scientific and the older generation too traditional. On second thought, guess everyone thinks the same since ages.

The journey of writing these stories began a year back. I started with "A Walk to Remember" to document my thoughts on my sanity. It did not take long, writing the first story of the collection was like an outburst of words, which came naturally. And then it became an everyday affair. Every story acted as a vent to the thousand scrambled messages that my Gemini mind brooded upon subconsciously.

There's a story behind every story and I feel that even that needs a mention here. The idea for "A Game of Chess" was born when I played chess with my friend in a cafeteria (I lost badly because she is a very good player). Amidst the game of chess played, the male protagonist remarks, "*I'm not suffering Trisha, I've never suffered all these years, someone long back taught me by example that it's very easy to be content with one's solitude. I've enjoyed mine all these years.*" That is what I tried to explore, solitude as against the "man is a social animal" adage.

The central theme of all the stories is very modern, something I have seen happening all around me. Another emotion that is prominent is the right balance between our individuality and the effect of people around us. The I vs everyone else. Sometimes we lose ourselves, when we change for people around us and sometimes it's just not possible to change someone. That's when acceptance steps in. Mrs. Seth accepts her destiny and surrenders herself completely. On the other hand, Joe's fixation (from "Achilles' Heel") when he says that "*he wants the power to kill the calm in Anusha's eyes*" leads him nowhere.

Why "Achilles' Heel"? I could not think of a better name to the story. When I started writing "Achilles' Heel", I named it as "Shades" by which I meant the shades in different people. The story is inspired by yet another conversation and a post-it note on which I wrote "Power to Kill" the moment those words were said over a cup of coffee. When I finished tying all the threads, the story was "Achilles' Heel". It symbolizes our inner weakness, that one thing which can give us away.

Everyone is in fact a product of their experiences, when Ananya remarks that "*Pain is the only pleasure in the world, this is the biggest paradox*", it's based on her experiences in life that changed her as a person. I have never studied philosophy or psychology, but the stories here touch upon many such conditions. So I can say that the things described here are a layman's approach to the deeper subjects.

Every man is a born philosopher and every person lives life based on his or her own set of ideals. When the guy from "A Clumsy Conversation" says that, "*people should believe me. What's the suspicion about? I trust people almost blindly. If that nice girl was to claim that she is a leading actress I would believe her.*" It is based on his own principles. There is no explanation to the behavior of any of the characters, from any of the stories. Infact, as an author even I am looking for some answers, for example, there could be a thousand reasons with Resha, from "Confessions", for her "not forever" philosophy with someone as statuesque like Arjun. It is open to the readers' interpretation. There are no morals drawn, no concluding remarks just a central idea around which a fictitious web is woven. I must also say that all the stories are written at one go. There was no going back to it, no revisions, and no embellishments. The words as they are printed are as they came to me. The only thing I changed in the final draft was the title. So the stories come in a form of a raw collection which I believe every individual can relate to and maybe the thoughts are something which everyone pondered upon sometime.

The reason I titled the whole collection *SHE* is obvious once one reads all the stories.

Lastly, I would like to say that I have tried desperately to hold my thoughts and keep every story as a "short story" and not a novella. I have many times turned pages to see where a short story ends and I hope the length of every story included here is just right to justify it being called a "short story".

I hope everyone enjoys reading them and takes a pause to think. The way I have when I wrote them.

Dixy Gandhi

Contents

A Walk to Remember

The fragrance of June always carried her to a different time, a different era altogether. It was a strange feeling of déjàvu. When she knew she had felt the way she felt now before, in the quiet of June, when the sun shone a little less bright, the wind refused to touch even a single leaf. The birds went all silent waiting for the storm to arrive. The stillness of the surrounding always raged a hurricane within her. When she desired to unshackle the invisible bonds and set herself free.

There were many things she could associate with the first rain, the things which she knew did not belong to this age, if she would have belonged to the school of orthodox, she could have easily attributed these strange thoughts to past life. But her education forced her to think otherwise, think rationally. The feel of unease refused to leave her alone. As she walked the lane from her home to the library, she tried various permutations to help her place the numerous objects her memory was throwing at her, things that the smell of dried leaves and the scorched road she was treading on imposed.

She tried singing, to help keep her mind away from the restlessness. The only songs she could remember were strange rhymes. The rhymes brought about another sensation. She remembered a cloth, like a fabric of a school uniform. It wasn't hers. She quite well remembered that her school uniform was blue. But the cloth she visualized now was a checkered one, in red and brown. It was so real that she could feel the softness of the fabric now. It made her rub her thumb with her index finger, the way she would have felt the fabric if it existed in real.

How she wished it would start raining at least, anything that would kill this serenity and her train of thoughts. She kept walking, increasing her pace, and wishing it would rain.

As the only measure left to canalize her thoughts to a more logical path, she started counting the steps she was taking, 1…2…3…

She had heard stories, the kind of tales that get allied with old cities, of old lovers waiting for ages to reunite in the woods calling for each other amidst the trees. Of soldiers wounded in war waiting for the doomsday crying for the loved ones they left behind to be in the war, of the ghost of an aged wrinkled woman traumatized by society waiting in a old broken house for her revenge. All these thoughts didn't make anything easier. The only thing they did was to envelop the tranquility with a blanket of sinister.

Suddenly she was thinking of the pattern of it all. It was 4 o'clock in the evening, but the streets were all deserted. On the long straight road ahead, she couldn't see a single soul. Strange, the only sound she could hear was her own voice in her head counting... 89...90...91.

And then the sound changed to her last night's lecture on child psychology. She could hear the hoarse voice of her professor mouthing the words, with his steel grey eyes staring not from his glasses but from above them as he enunciated the words that pierced directly from the sharpness of his eyes to the eyes of anyone who dared to hold his stare. Unfortunately, the professor chose her as his subject when he explained the following: "Repression is one of the most haunting concepts in psychology. Something shocking happens, and the mind pushes it into some inaccessible corner of the unconscious mind. Later, the memory may emerge into consciousness". Sometimes the look of his eyes forced one to believe that he knew something more than what met the average eye.

He continued looking at her even after he finished reciting the Freudian concept of repressed memories. And another memory fluttered its wings, as she continued holding his stare, his eyes were a gateway, the midnight black pupil set as a concentric circle to the halo of steel grey went deeper in shade, if it was possible to go in a darker shade of black, and she saw a house. She knew of her presence in the class but was also aware of her presence outside the medieval house built in red bricks with an iron gate to guard it. A house located at the corner. She knew if she turned the corner, she would be transported to a different land.

"You understand. Don't you?" The hoarse voice brought her back to class.

She was counting again 101…102…103.

The road seemed to be longer than everyday, it refused to end. The weather had turned into a threatening quiet. She heard a cuckoo, maybe perched on one of the trees that lined the road, and wished that it rain, if only it rained. It would destroy the silence, make kids come out and play and wash away her strange thoughts. If only it rained…

She didn't believe in re-incarnations, for the sake of God, she didn't even believe in God. From the time she remembered she had a happy childhood, so these things couldn't be attributed to her past. She needed an immediate answer.

The library was still a long way ahead. She had decided to walk today to kill time. Walking in a small hill station with beautiful scenery had its own advantage. Many a times she had walked the same way chatting with her friends and the distance had shortened. But today it refused to end.

She tried to fight the bizarre thoughts. She heard her professor again. When he had remarked in one of his classes, "Don't fight your inner self, the sooner you accept yourself, the faster you reach your goals. You can't change the person you are, the person that makes you is deeply ingrained inside, if you wish to change it, you are going to loose. Don't fight yourself. Accept yourself." This particular thought was obviously from his school of thoughts, distributed among the class in the form of complementary education, the way you get on the house drinks from your favorite restaurant with the food you ordered.

A voice countered his particular quotation. "Isn't it better to go down fighting than accepting something you want to change?"

She realized that the voice was hers when she met the professor's stare. All thoughts of a fight left her brain as he stared. He didn't reply. And she didn't force for an answer.

"Okay professor I'll try to accept," She said aloud to herself, now as she continued walking the lane.

"So first things first, who am I?"

"I'm a person at peace with myself. I am having a good education. I've a great family. I do miss them at times but then I've nice friends. There's nothing that I lack in my life. I have a secure future, so that's not bothering me really."

"So what is bothering me?"

"This road, this silence, and these bizarre thoughts, right now it's like I am alone in this world. I would just like to scream out aloud just to make sure the city is alive. Maybe I should knock the next door I see to make sure that human beings reside here."

"They do. See the little boy standing on the window."

She just waved at him and he waved back.

"So people exist. What next?"

"Don't know. Let's see what I have in store for today."

"Well I'm headed to the library. I've to study for tomorrow's exam. I'll come back by 9 o'clock. Go to Mall Road, hang out with my friends. Walk my way back home. Have food, and sleep. Nothing beats an uncomplicated life."

"Did you just say uncomplicated? You could have said "simple". Why did you complicate it?"

"Wait. I can feel something again. Who am I talking to? Is there someone inside me? God…No… can't be… I can't be a MPD. Who the hell are you?"

The professor spoke again in his croaky voice, "The causes of multiple personality disorder (MPD) have not been identified, but are theoretically linked with the interaction of overwhelming stress, traumatic antecedents, insufficient childhood nurturing, and an innate ability to dissociate memories or experiences from consciousness. Prolonged childhood abuse is frequently a factor, with a very high percentage of patients reporting documented abuse often confirmed by objective evidence."

"No… it can't be me. What are the symptoms? Quick… try and recall the symptoms. The psychology book flashed before her eyes as she tried to recall:

> Individuals with MPD demonstrate a variety of symptoms with wide fluctuations across time; symptoms can include:

1. Multiple mannerisms, attitudes and beliefs that are dissimilar to each other (No, I've the same beliefs I had as a kid.) Crossed—not applicable.
2. Headaches and other body pains (I do have headache, but that's because I don't eat well.) but serious issue should be considered.
3. Distortion or loss of subjective time—none that I recall of.
4. Depersonalization—well no.
5. Amnesia—no.
6. Depression—well no. Why should I be?"

"Such a relief I am not a MPD."

She continued walking. A smile escaped her lips as she laughed on herself, for being so paranoid. If anyone could just see her now, walking alone. Laughing to herself. Revising her notes.

"Oh... I'm going insane."

The cuckoo cooed again.

"Is it following me? Okay, mate, come along."

She tried imitating his voice and then for next 5 minutes she replied to him. She imitated every cry of the cuckoo and he replied. They were talking in a secret code, both failed to understand. For a while she wasn't alone. And she felt jubilant.

"Just a 10 minutes walk and I would reach the library. Thanks a lot cuckoo for saving me from going insane."

If she had believed in God she would have thanked him for saving her from insanity. But she didn't. She believed that God was just a way of not accepting blame for one's own actions. How can everything be put to kismet? At least a person should own his thoughts.

So she tried to own her thoughts. She saw the white tourist vehicle approaching her and it all came to her.

The quietness of the weather, the orange aura the sun had spread on everything around her. The voice of the cuckoo, and her inability to move an inch as the car hit her. It wasn't déjàvu. But she knew it was going to happen.

Hell... she knew since the time she felt uncomfortable in this weather and that was very long ago.

She could see it all again, the checkered cloth, the house and a pair of blue eyes staring at her. The first few drops of rain that she felt on her face. And then it rained.

She could still hear the drops against the glass of the window. Her head ached as she pushed herself against the pillows. A low moan escaped her lips as she tried to open her eyes.

"Relax, you're still hurt." She heard a voice from her dreams.

How can she forget? The cloth, the house was followed by a voice. A voice matured with age, a voice that always soothed her.

She opened her eyes to find herself in a room which wasn't hers. Before she could use the over used phrase "where am I?"

The voice spoke again. "I hope you're feeling good now. We were scared. I'd just inform my son."

The voice hurried out of the room, before she could see her.

She was back in five minutes with a glass of water. And she could immediately recognize the blue eyes. The eyes lined by wrinkles of old age, and filled with compassion.

"I know you." She said.

The eyes showed a question which the old lady didn't mouth.

"What are you doing here?" she kept on speaking as if in a trance and the questioned look in the old eyes deepened.

The old woman approached her and her wizened hand took hers.

"You just relax miss. You're obviously in a state of shock."

The old lady started walking out of the room, as she called her name.

"Ailsa."

The old woman turned in a state of shock. The obvious question in her eyes was, "how do you know my name?"

She didn't know herself.

"Ailsa Cullen" she said again, and the shock in the old eyes deepened.

The old lady's posture showed that she was scared and would have run away if another person won't have entered the room at that instant.

Whatever she did was in state of semi-consciousness. She knew things but she didn't know why she was saying them with confidence.

"Frank, this girl..." the old lady started. But Frank cut her off.

"I'm really sorry for the little mishap. Actually it was my driver."

She just nodded.

"No Frank, it wasn't your driver. It was me." She replied. She had a smile on her face, a complacent smile. They were not formally introduced yet and she used his name with an unexplainable ease.

Even Frank was a bit surprised.

"Anyway, I'm Frank Cullen," he said and then gestured towards the old woman to add, "and she is my mother Ailsa."

She took his extended hand and winked at Ailsa, who was nearly frozen.

Everything made sense in a way now.

She didn't know what made her steal a glance at her watch. But Frank offered as a means of explanation for the loss of time.

"You were unconscious for nearly an hour. Nothing to worry though, the doctor said you are just in a state of shock."

"Why didn't you act this responsible last time?" she asked

"What?"

It all made sense to her now.

"Trust me, I've wasted many years trying to analyze the strange sensations, I didn't believe in it all but now I do."

"Are you still in shock?" Frank asked her.

"How old are you?" she asked instead.

"43. But what's that got to do with anything?"

She perhaps knew if she pushed this too far she may be thrown outside the house. But she didn't care. She was suddenly filled with a rare kind of courage.

"I'm 23."

Frank didn't say anything. He just shrugged as if to say "so?"

Ailsa was still frozen in her place. The old lady perhaps was saying a quiet prayer in her mind. She had heard a lot about the tales of Indian magic and was wondering if she was subjected to one of those tricks or a bigger con.

Frank on the other hand was perhaps waiting for her to announce her departure. But she was in no hurry.

She was thinking, putting all the pieces together of her great puzzle, and it all made sense to her. She looked around the room to see some luggage with the "British Airways" tag on it. The ways of the universe made her smile.

"How long are you guys in India?" she asked.

"We just arrived this morning, we were coming from the airport, when our hired car hit you" Frank explained. "I hope you're fine" He added as an afterthought just because she was acting really weird.

"If you can give your address, I'll make sure my driver escorts you back home" Ailsa spoke this time. Maybe she just wanted to get rid of this strange Indian girl as soon as possible.

"Oh sure" she replied. "But before I go I just want to get some things out of my system. Things that are troubling me a lot since I remember."

So she got up from the bed and started pacing the room. Frank pitied the girl for her loss of good sense after the accident. Ailsa was quite convinced that she was the Indian witch.

"Frank, you remember the church you played bagpipe for?" she asked him.

Now, even Frank was confounded. He just nodded.

"And you remember the girl in pigtails, always in the front row of the pew?" she asked again.

"No I don't. Listen, what are you getting at?" Now he was loosing his patience.

She didn't pay any attention to his impatience as she continued, "You don't? She always used to sit at the aisle seat just right to where you stood playing the bagpipe?" she tried to make him recall.

Frank remembered now. "Yes I do, what about her?"

"What else you remember about her?" she asked again.

"Don't know it's a long time back. You want me to call the doctor again." Frank was now sure that she had lost her mind.

She just smiled.

"I'll tell you, Frank. She stayed in the red bungalow at the end of your lane. She went to the same school as you. And the day you led the church choir she was right there. You winked at her at the end of the prayers. You said you'll meet her one Sunday, and the same evening you knocked her in a hit and run case just outside the church. You didn't even wait to see whom you had hit. Why didn't you act responsible then?"

Frank was confused. He didn't reply.

"I haven't been to Scotland." She continued. "But for 23 long years I have lived in the memory of the tunes you played on the bagpipe, the memories of the traditional attire you wore with the checkered skirt. The memories of me waiting near the Church and wondering if you would come before the rain, scared of the stillness around and waiting for you." She continued. "I haven't been to any church since I remember just because seeing one even from a distance makes me feel uncomfortable."

"All because of you" she accused.

Frank was speechless.

She gathered her belongings and came out of the room.

The cuckoo cooed again and interrupted her thoughts.

Now she could see the library. She increased her pace.

"Nice story, but I need a better one." She thought as she climbed the stairs of the library. "Enough of owning my thoughts, I think I need to focus on my exam tomorrow."

The walk ended as she entered the library. And then it started raining, she didn't feel the drops on the glass pane, as she engrossed herself in the quietness of the library and her books. She also missed the white tourist vehicle that raced past the library nearly hitting a tree. And she didn't even look up, as the man in the tourist vehicle closed his eyes momentarily in remembrance of an old painful reminiscence.

A Game of Chess

Trisha met her best friend–solitude for the first time at an age of 15. Till that age, her elder sister was her best ally. There were many memories related to her sister from their childhood. Michelle was just 3 years elder to Trisha but she always treated her with motherly concern.

They spent their childhood in a quiet lane of Goa, where they lived in an ancestral home. The beach wasn't far and as kids both of them had spent hours building sandcastles there.

Trisha always concentrated on spread of her house. Her own little sand work had a small cottage located at the foothills surrounded by twigs picked from nearby trees that acted as her garden. She would create a small pathway that would lead to the sea. Some days she would build a huge house replicating her own home with a road turning many a times to lead to the sea. All her dreams were centred on the ocean. She never really wanted to get out of the place she had grown up in.

Michelle was different. Her display of art on the beach always included a castle with tall walls depicting the medieval age. She always pictured herself in one of the tall towers of the castle, waiting to be rescued. She enjoyed being with her little sister, encouraging her in every endeavour, but at the same time she also missed something, something she couldn't name. And then at the age of 18, Michelle went away to study. Initially, Trisha enjoyed the long letters her sister sent to her describing her life in the new city. Her heart went out to the love she felt, when Michelle would send her gifts saving from her meagre pocket money.

For two years, she day-dreamed about the life her sister was leading in another city while she continued living in the same old house. She lived every exciting moment with Michelle. She would wait eagerly for Michelle to return during vacations so that they could continue their fun together. Trisha didn't even realize when Michelle out grew the games they played when they role-played as different people, imitating lives of everyone from their school teacher, to the famous tinsel town actor.

Trisha was a fun loving person. As a school kid her parents were many a times embarrassed by the complaints her school kept on sending because of her naughtiness. She still laughed at the memory when as an eighth grader she had mustered up the courage to plan an outing during school time when her group of friends had run away from school all the way to the beach. The whole plan was masterminded by her solely and she had to bear the brunt of it all when all her friends chickened out the next day and blamed her in entirety.

Gradually without her realizing, she changed. By the time she reached college, she had grown up to be a quiet kid with few friends around her.

Around the same time her parents shifted to a bigger city, Michelle came back to stay with them after a gap of five years. But the bond was severed. Trisha could no longer talk that freely with her. They were now two strangers living in the same house, they still shared the laughs but something had changed.

Trisha missed the place she had grown up in. She had turned into a recluse. She had never ever analyzed her behaviour but her family did a good job of it. She was the one not known by any of her relatives abroad. She was the one sitting quietly in a corner at all the family functions. And she was the one always called as the shy one by everyone who met her. Michelle was the extrovert.

Gradually, things had stopped to affect her in any way. Michelle got married when Trisha turned 21 and was still in college. Trisha was the only one without a teary eye at the wedding. She didn't know why she didn't feel like crying when almost everyone around her was. But that was the first time she knew she had to run away.

As soon as she completed her education, she moved to Shimla, a place miles away from her home town. Her only contact with her family now were the weekly phone calls and the bi-annual visits, the ones she tried to put off the most. She was at peace. She finally understood what George Burns meant when he said, "Happiness is having a large, loving, caring, close-knit family in another city."

The Trisha inside her longed to return to her childhood, when life was spent lazing on the beach. And the Trisha of the day rebelled to the mountains. Her life changed, she only knew selected people around her. Her days were spent working as a lecturer in the City College and evenings in waiting for the sun to set, for a new day to begin. Life wasn't a bed of roses but it wasn't difficult either, anyways she was not complaining. She had already spent a year this way, and was pretty happy with herself leading a mundane life.

And then she befriended someone she saw many a times in the coffee shop. Lately, Trisha had started stopping for coffee on her way back from work. Just enjoying a cup of coffee alone gave her a different high.

It all started from the day when she spotted the Café outlet while returning from work and remembered the time when Michelle had come home in her vacations and taken her to the café outlet back home. It was the first time in Trisha's life when she was introduced to the concept of hanging out at cafeterias for coffee and fun. Michelle had narrated many anecdotes of her new life in a bigger city over that one cup of mocha they shared then. She entered the café one day and from then on, it was a routine.

Initially, Trisha just went in for a cup of coffee and actually enjoyed the ambience spending an hour just looking at people around her. Next day she went in for a quick snack and a cup of coffee. After that she started carrying the book she was reading currently and would spend hours together there.

It was a Sunday when Trisha met him for the first time. She got up late that day and with absolutely no work at hand and no will to stay at home, she had snatched her bag which was thrown carelessly after coming back from the café the day before and gone to the coffee house for breakfast. With her hair oiled and wearing the work clothes of the day before she wasn't a pretty sight, but she didn't care. The café was pretty much vacant. While she was waiting for her food to arrive, she remembered that she still had her book in the bag. It was more than half done, so she decided to finish it over breakfast.

Fifteen minutes later, she was deeply engrossed in her book, when someone interrupted her.

"You like chess?"

At first she wasn't sure if the words were meant for her. But then she looked up to see a lanky maybe teenager looking at her. Trisha looked at him with questioned eyes. She had a hard time coming out of the aura of the book.

He pointed to the title. For a moment, Trisha didn't even remember the name of the book she was reading, she was absorbed in the characters and had to re-read the name to recall.

"Not really, I like reading." She replied.

"Reading about the game too I guess—*Shatranj ke Khiladi.*" He repeated the name of the book.

With no words to answer, Trisha just shrugged.

"I like chess too, but don't usually find company to play."

Trisha didn't know what to say so she just smiled.

"Would you like to play?" He asked again.

"What? Here?"

"I'll be back", he said and ran out of the café before she had a chance to answer. Within minutes he was back with a chess set.

"White or black?" he asked without looking up.

Now it had been years since Trisha played chess, but she found herself saying "black". At least this way she won't be making the first move. She smiled at the idea; anyways she had not made the first move.

So that was the first day they both played chess in the café, the game lasted for about 3 hours and few cups of coffee. It ended with Trisha saying, "checkmate" and not actually knowing if she won or was allowed to win.

"Not bad" he said, "by the way I'm Rocky. I'm here for vacations and see you here everyday so guessed you are a local but then you don't look like a local." He added.

Trisha was in no mood to befriend, for her he was just a brain competing against her in the game, the way she played against the computer as an adolescent, not giving up till she won. And the computer had never initiated a pep talk after the game!

She didn't reply.

"Another game?" he asked.

"I think I'll go back to my book." Trisha replied picking up her book for affect.

He didn't force and walked out of the café. Trisha went back to reading.

Next day when she returned from college and entered the café he was already there. He waved at her and Trisha joined him out of politeness. By the time she seated herself; he had taken out the chess-set and was arranging the pieces. Another 5 hours both played chess and she won again.

"You're not good for my self-image." He exclaimed at the end of the game. Trisha still was not sure about the authenticity of her victory. This time he didn't wait for any chat and was out of the café immediately after the game.

The next day, they played two games in a row and Trisha won both. He told her about himself during the game without her asking. He was 16 and was in town to visit his grandparents. He never asked anything about her and she never told him anything.

Over a period of two weeks, Trisha had lost the count of the games she won, but he never gave up. Instead, he had started putting up a brave fight which had resulted in long games that lasted more than four to five hours. In the meantime, she also learned that he lived in Goa with his parents, she never told him that she belonged to the same place. He would talk about himself in the course of the game but leave as soon as Trisha said "checkmate". Then one day he said he was leaving. His vacation was over. They both said their byes and he was gone.

Trisha's life was back to what it was before the phase of chess.

And then the letters arrived.

It was just another day for her, when she arrived at the café and the man who served her order also gave her a brown envelope. She found a small note inside with only a few lines scribbled on it. The lines thanked her for a wonderful time and also placed a bet on her next win. Trisha couldn't help smiling at the innocence of it all. Another letter arrived a week later and she found some pictures of the beaches she had grown up in. Behind every picture was a detailed account and background of the particular scenery, all scrawled in a near legible hand. The letter also said that, he wasn't sure if Trisha had ever visited a beach or not and so he wanted her to get a feel of his life at the beach.

The letters were becoming a weekly affair. The next one described at length his new life at college. He wondered if Trisha would ever like to visit Goa in her vacation and if she did, would she meet him. The one after that gave a brief account of the annual sports day in his college and how he had reached the finals in the chess competition. Trisha was living his life with him the way she had spent her childhood living Michelle's life with her.

The first few letters had a return address of a P.O. Box with the name "Rocky" written in capitals on the other side of envelope. But when Trisha didn't reply for a month, he stopped writing the address. It was just a one way conversation from then on. Trisha would arrive at the café and twice a week, she would receive the brown envelope with her coffee. She never thought of replying. She would read the letter and then fold it neatly to put it in her book.

Six months passed, Trisha had a written account of everything happening in his life. He never cared to ask her about her life. Maybe he knew she would never reply. He wrote about every single detail in his life to her. He told Trisha how scared he was when his mother got sick. He wrote about how alone he felt because no one else would understand how he feels seeing his mother on bed. Trisha went back to the time when she had suffered each and every moment with her mother in her illness. Trisha's mother didn't survive her illness. It was long time back, but his words brought back everything.

In one of his letters he wrote that he was getting addicted to writing to her and asked if she felt the same way about reading his letters. Trisha didn't. She was having a hard time distinguishing habit and addiction. Her job, her daily coffee at the café, the novels she read were things done out of habit, she didn't know where the letters fitted in. They lived their life together in the letters.

Trisha was yet to scrutinize her relationship. When they met in the café he was just a kid she played chess with. When the letters started arriving, she just read them because she relived her childhood naughtiness in his anecdotes. Her childhood was still playing on those beaches he described so vividly, she had piled her sorrows, love and tears on the sand of those beaches, the sand somewhere had a part of the castles she had built on them.

The hill station was a small one, the kind where everyone knew everyone and the café was frequented by quite a few people. She had never paid any heed to the local gossips. And then she heard the latest doing the rounds. It was about a lecturer in the town having a romantic escapade with a kid. Her colleagues had passed on the information to her in the juiciest manner possible. The lecturer in question was called a cradle snatcher and all other names one could associate with things like that.

Trisha took a leave from her job the next day and went on to visit her sister. It was the first vacation in her three years at the City College. Michelle never asked her anything. Within a month, she was tired of running away from things and she knew she had to return. She went back to her job. The gossips had mellowed down. The people at the café told her with a sly smile that in her absence the kid she played chess with had been there and had left few letters for her. Trisha asked them to repost it to the returning address.

After that no letters came and with passage of time the old town forgot about everything that had happened.

Trisha continued living there. Her family had resigned her to her fate after her father died. Michelle moved to live in US with her family. Even she had given up on her after her every effort of compelling Trisha to settle down went in vain. She mailed her initially, but then that stopped too.

Trisha was enjoying her seclusion. Years rolled by and with them the reminiscence of her happy childhood faded away too. She still worked at the City College. All these years had added a few grey strands to her hair, a PhD and Masters to her qualification and uncountable books in her personal library. Except for some brief pangs sometimes which she attributed to the onset of middle age nothing was amiss from her life.

The town looked at her with a renewed respect the way one would look at a nun. The old scandals were buried. People around her now gave her a familiar smile when they passed her. The café had a place reserved for her. The same place where long back she had played chess with someone she had hard time remembering now. The staff served her coffee without her asking for it and no one disturbed her as she read for hours in the café.

Then one day, she caught a glimpse of someone she thought she knew at the café. She saw him smiling at her as she passed her way to her daily spot. He was a man around 30 years of age working on his laptop, dressed formally but the eyes that never left her right from the moment she entered the café to the time she opened her book to read had a mischievous glint in them. Trisha chose to ignore him.

"Would you like to play?" a deep voice asked and Trisha looked up to see the same man at her table. He looked familiar. Recognition hit her, but she didn't smile. He seated himself opposite her and opened the chess board. He placed it between them with the white pieces facing Trisha.

"I'm tired of making all the first moves", he offered as a means of explanation.

So Trisha moved her King's Pawn two squares forward. He responded by moving his King's Pawn.

"It's nice to meet you again." He said. She smiled.

Trisha brought out her bishop in her second move.

He brought his knight out.

"I wrote to you, you never replied." He said.

This time she brought her knight out.

He brought his queen right to the last diagonal square, where Trisha could easily take her with her knight in a move. But she didn't take the bait. Instead she did the "Castling" and moved her king to a safer place. He smiled.

"You know, I came here again but you had gone into hiding". He said.

"I was on leave" Trisha replied. It seemed ages ago, like all of it didn't matter anymore.

"I heard that." He was on an aggressive mode, but just listening to her voice softened him. He retreated the queen.

Trisha moved her rook one place sideways. And he knew that she was just playing around the pieces.

"I'm sorry for whatever that happened then." He said. Trisha looked at him with questioned eyes.

"I know why you took that leave." He added. Trisha was still toying with the pawns without forming a winning strategy. Something inside her had somersaulted and she had no idea how to react to the situation she found herself in.

"I was very young then and I agree I made some stupid moves, but that was no ones business but ours."

He moved his knight and captured one of her pawns. Trisha didn't flinch. He smiled at an old memory; he remembered how years back it was an uphill task to even capture her one pawn. She never believed in the piece for piece theory and never let the opponent capture even a pawn from her side, unless it was an absolute give away.

Trisha retaliated in the next move by taking his knight.

The board was getting vacant and he still had no idea how she would react to what he had to say.

"I still live in Goa", he said and placed a postcard on the table which had a picture of an old albeit beautiful house. The picture was taken in the manner that the sea was seen at the backyard, as if the house was floating on the sea. "This is where I live" he added.

Trisha just glanced at the picture.

"That's my house; my father sold it to some Richard Babel years back," she said as a matter of fact.

He smiled and extended his hand. "I'm Richard Babel".

They didn't play for a while and both of them were looking at the board confounded.

"I always knew you belong to the beach, you don't fit here. When I saw you here, I thought how at peace you are but then something was wrong. Your skin has this permanent tan that only life at beach offers; you lack the blush of the hills."

No one had ever got this personal with her so Trisha didn't know how to react.

She saw a way to attack his king, but she also knew he would easily save him; still she carried out the attack.

"Check", she said.

He retaliated by taking her bishop that had attacked his king. He didn't want to disarm her completely but she had regained her composure and was playing quite aggressively.

They kept playing quietly for a while. Trisha was on a spree as she captured his rook and two pawns. She remembered the way he used to panic, when he saw her winning, years back. She looked up at him to catch any such sign but he kept smiling.

"So how have you been?" she asked as she advanced her knight on a capturing spree from the left to the centre of the board as she took another of his pawns. It was the first time that she had asked him anything about him; he took it as a progress in their association.

"Trisha, I'm not suffering", he replied. "I've never suffered all these years, someone long back taught me by example that it's very easy to be content with ones solitude. I've enjoyed mine all these years."

She didn't reply and contemplated her next move as she waited for him to play his turn. It was the first time that he had used her name and it felt strange.

"But things have to stop at some place." He continued as he conquered her knight before it could pose any more danger.

"You've to come out of the closet someday and fight your own battles; no one does that for you." He continued.

"Not even a knight" he showed her the just captured piece and smiled.

Trisha moved a pawn that left his king defenseless in the corner. He brought his queen there.

"Check", he said.

She moved the king out a place because there was no place else to move.

"Like I said, you've to come out of the closet," he repeated and smiled.

They sat in silence for a while as a thousand thoughts raced through Trisha's mind.

"Your turn", he reminded her.

"I don't know what to say," she said out loud and he knew he was going to win. He just grinned.

"This time you don't have a say, I am not a kid anymore. I can't change anything that happened back then but I can just show you a way to end your reclusion."

Trisha didn't look up.

He pushed the picture of their house towards her.

She just glanced at it and again concentrated on the board and moved her king one place backward as all her other pieces were already lost in gambit or locked at strategic locations.

He immediately brought his rook from the other end.

"Checkmate", he said as Trisha picked up the picture from the table.

Inked on Me

He was 16 when the idea first struck him, after that it had become a fixation; Brendan was totally obsessed with the thought. He had spent hours in drawing sketches of his creative designs. Designs for something he wanted inked on him.

He knew he wasn't a sheep; whatever was going to be etched on him forever had to be unique. He toyed with many a things right from animals, birds, Chinese alphabets to abstract art. And then he realized that it was him, if he died under unexplainable circumstances, between people he didn't know, his tattoo would be a mark of his identity. If he was somehow mummified and exhumed ages later among strange people of the future then, among someone who may carry an iota of his DNA, his tattoo would be him, his personality.

"I am not an artist; I can't produce beautiful, breath-taking art work", he thought. "But then my body isn't a canvas either, I don't want the person who exhumes me to remark, "Hey, look this one has a whole crap of paintings done on him, bet he didn't find a paper".

"I'm not God-father either and I don't want to carry any souvenirs." But the idea still refused to go away.

He came home and announced, "I'm going to get a tattoo."

His mother had a fit. "You'll regret it", she said. His father was as usual indifferent.

His best friend said "way to go, mate". So he went.

The only problem was that the parlor refused to insert a needle into someone below 18 without parental consent. He was unaware of the legalities of the issue, so the next thing he did was take advantage of his 6' 2" frame and his genes to grow a beard and dressed himself in his best grown-up clothes, donned an ascent and went to another parlor.

An hour later he was out with a red flushed face, a sore wrist and his real short best friend jumping like a monkey behind him, over his shoulder shouting, "That was cool, Man".

And he was strutting ahead with pride. He wanted to shout out to the next man he saw on street, let everyone know that he had finally done it. He had a tattoo. He felt like a grown-up. Brendan had heard his father boast about the moment when he had grown up in a day. It was after Brendan's grandfather died in a mining accident, his father had to shoulder all the responsibilities at the age of 12. "That was the day, I grew up son, seeing the corpse of my beloved father," he would often remark. Brendan wanted to scream out to his dad, "see dad, I grew up too, I didn't need death to mature me."

The first thing he did after getting out of the parlor was meeting his girlfriend. He had kept her in dark for too long.

"I got a tattoo done," he announced. They had a daily ritual of chatting for an hour standing under the banyan tree that had marked their introduction and courtship. As a shy ten year old, Brendan had lost control of his cycle and hit the same banyan tree and a bold girl had come forward to nurse his bruises. He had reached the same place the very next day after the accident to give that helping girl a note of thanks and a sweet box on insistence of his mother. That little incident had marked their friendship.

They would chat under the tree unaware of the minutes slipping to hours. The tree now also bore a tattoo expertly crafted on its trunk bearing the names of Brendan and his young friend.

"Did it hurt?" his girlfriend asked him eyeing with suspicion the bandage clad wrist.

"Not as much," he lied.

"What does it look like?" she asked again.

"Wait and watch", he winked.

So they waited for an hour as per the instruction and after that it looked scary with all the tortured skin swelled up to show its displeasure at being subjected to assault in such a brutal manner.

"It must have pained", she exclaimed.

"No it didn't", he lied again. He won't have accepted it in front of her even in his dreams the excruciating pain he felt.

"What does it mean?" she asked.

"It means something in my mother tongue."

"What?" she insisted again.

So he told her. She wasn't happy with it, but she smiled. What is inevitable is to be accepted with grace.

"You really mean it, don't you?" she asked.

He just shrugged.

She knew he meant the phrase he had got carved on himself so valiantly; it was his motto in life, a fuel that had driven him in moments of crisis. In fact, she had been attracted to him for that one reason, for his self reliance, for his knack of standing for things he believed in, for people he believed in and if no one did, he would stand alone. He had inked it on himself as a reminder, "come what may, I can face it. I don't need support for something I know is right, even if the world turns its back on me, I'll still stand alone". And that were exactly the words he got on himself, "Stand alone" carved in bold italics below a miniature lion.

She kept smiling as he narrated the whole experience in the parlor.

"It was fun", he narrated. "The place is like a dungeon. I don't know why the owner has it made to that effect. It was full of creepy people too."

She kept nodding.

"The guy before me had his full hand covered with tattoos. Freaky!" Brendan exclaimed.

"Guess he wanted something on his back now. It freaks me actually, I mean a little thing is like okay, like you try something out but getting the whole skin covered with different animals, symbols, daggers, modern art goes kind of over board. Does it not?"

"And yours doesn't?" she asked.

"I don't think so", Brendan replied with a shrug.

"Isn't it facing the wrong way?" she asked. He didn't understand her.

"I mean the words are facing your side, I thought the tattoo is for the world to see, so shouldn't the words be facing outwards, like you extend your hand and people read it?" she asked.

He inspected the wound on the inner side of his wrist. The words were an arch, facing him, the way he could read it, not the world.

"You want to read what it says? Maybe touch it?" he asked her, extending his hand with the palm facing upwards.

She wanted to, but she had to cross her way and stand next to him to be able to read it properly and to stroke her finger over the wound. He smiled.

"See, I may stand alone, but if someone wants to come along, he has to do so as a friend. Stand by my side to comprehend my philosophy. The tattoo is for me, if the world wants a look at it, it has to be on my side, with me not against me."

"Philosophical", she exclaimed.

"But the truth", he argued.

"So tell me how much did it honestly hurt?" she asked again with a smirk.

"Why do you keep asking that? I said it does not." Brendan lied again.

"Well, I just wanted to measure the extent you can go to get it etched on you and the people around you, your philosophy."

"Well, honestly it hurts just a bit", Brendan confessed sheepishly.

"Maybe I should get one done too." She stated and Brendan was confused.

"I don't know you are just not the type."

"And what type do you think I am?"

"The puritan".

She laughed, stroked his tattoo once more and said in a low voice, "I wish and hope that you had not got it done, anyway I got to go."

She walked away, before Brendan could say a word.

Brendan moved out of his house to attend college in other city miles away with a multitude of instructions from his mother, repetitive looks of apathy from his father and the rhythmic slapping on the back from his best friend with "will miss you, bro". College was a welcome change but what was left behind was left behind. Not that he cared, he could adapt to any situation and that he did magnificently.

The distance severed the bond between Brendan and his best friend. "You never call", he told Brendan and gradually they stopped talking. His girlfriend left him to do a course in hospitality in another country without telling him. He laughed at the irony when he knew.

The connection with his family was never so great. He found himself all alone in a new city. He did make some new friends but for most of the time he was alone.

He graduated decently in four years, got a great job and was doing great for his age. Years changed him from an over-confident teenager to a practical man. The full sleeve shirts covered the tattoo for most part of the days, and he didn't mind flaunting it on other days.

"Oh, you have a tattoo", a colleague remarked on one of their official trips as they sat next to each other on flight.

"Yeah, something I got as a kid" he replied.

"A lion" he laughed and Brendan smiled back.

"Être seul" the colleague read it aloud. "Ever regret it; everyone does stupid things as kids".

"No, I don't. I still mean it."

"Well, in today's world, you can hardly stand alone, it's all team spirit."

"I try to", Brendan replied.

"Really?" The colleague remarked and Brendan just shrugged.

"Well, there's a thin line between loneliness and solitude." Brendan explained. The colleague kept looking at him like he was from another planet.

"Loneliness is imposed by society, it kills you and solitude is self inflicted. I enjoy my solitude."

"Philosophical," the colleague remarked and went off to sleep. They did not talked again for the rest of the trip.

"You would like something to drink Sir?" the air hostess asked. Brendan was resting with his eyes closed after his colleague had abruptly closed their conversation but the voice sounded familiar.

He opened his eyes to see his one time girlfriend standing before him with a tray of soft drinks.

She smiled.

He knew she had recognized him but he didn't say a word. As soon as the flight landed and the crew descended, he went after her.

"Should I assume that you haven't recognized me and reintroduce myself?" he asked her.

"No one can forget you Brendan", she replied.

"Thanks", he mouthed and invited her for coffee.

"Thanks for the acknowledgement," he said as they sat in the coffee house. She smiled.

He right away wanted to ask her the reason for her going away but he didn't know how to.

"So you are doing well," he said instead.

But she knew he deserved certain explanations, "You never needed anyone Brendan, I could have dragged whatever we had for as long as I wanted and you won't have noticed. I admired your sense of self worth as an adolescent but it was turning into indifference. I had to leave. I needed to feel important and you always wanted to be left alone. I couldn't penetrate the walls you had around you."

She didn't give him any chance to explain and he couldn't have explained anyway because he didn't understand her, all the stuff she said was out of nowhere for him.

Brendan reached home and called his best friend.

"Long time!" his friend exclaimed in the same over excited manner he talked as a teenager.

"I need to know something," Brendan said

"Anything for you, friend", he replied.

"Did you ever think I was indifferent to you?" Brendan asked.

There was a long pause before he asked, "Why do you want to know?" so Brendan narrated the whole thing at the airport to him.

"When was the last time you called me Bro?" he asked.

Brendan had a hard time remembering so he remained silent.

"That answers your question", he replied.

Brendan was about to hang up but he continued.

"It all started with the tattoo you got".

"What about it?" Brendan asked confused.

"We've grown up together Brendan, I know you keep to yourself, you're not that expressive as I am, you may not say it but you love me as a brother. But the day you got that tattoo, I wondered if you really need me. She also felt the same."

"But I never meant it to be like that", Brendan retaliated.

"Everyone is not Einstein bro; we normal folks take things at face value".

Brendan returned home with a plethora of thoughts running through his mind. In an act of exasperation, he even rubbed the damn thing off himself. He slept thinking of the people he had met and left over the last few years. And then he dreamed of it.

In his dream, the words on his hand were dancing and then he saw the blood oozing out of it. Then he saw the words turn into fluid and the fluid enter his veins to make a trail over to his heart. All along the words hummed out loud like a chant. He saw her waving goodbye to him. He woke up with a start.

Good sense returned the next day for a while. He was denied the promotion he was counting on. "We need someone who takes everyone along as the company makes progress. Lone wolves can't progress." The President said in his opening speech.

"I am sorry", his colleague remarked with a slap on his shoulder.

"Don't be." Brendan replied. He quit his job and returned to his hometown.

The city welcomed him with open arms. He called his best friend and informed him about his arrival.

"That's great, how long will you be here?"

"Indefinitely", his best friend gave him a look of disbelief.

"I lost my job", Brendan explained.

"You of all people!" his best friend exclaimed. He went on blabbering for a fair amount of time. "You are one of the smartest guys in town. Why would anyone want to lose you? You were doing well, weren't you? Sure you were. What happened?"

Finally Brendan had to stop him. "I quit". And then Brendan explained at length the events that led to his decision.

"Here" his best friend handed him a brochure of a laser removal centre in uptown.

"I don't need it", Brendan replied.

"Why are you so adamant? You were sixteen then, just get the damn thing off and lead a normal life. We are in a corporate world bro and this thing doesn't fit in." He tried to give him a piece of his mind.

Brendan eyed the tattoo again, getting rid of it would mean going against the very meaning of it.

"I won't, I better stand by it".

Things didn't get any better. He started his own business manufacturing custom-made stuff for people, a place where he ran things his way. He was still standing opposite the world and thought that no one comprehended him not even the person he had explained his way of living in detail to.

A girl frequented his store; she had ordered many custom made things for herself right from Tees, cups, watches to coasters. Everything had her face on it. It made him sick. For him, it was narcissi, but it was business. So he catered to her orders.

"Oh! you have a tattoo", she exclaimed one day.

"Many people do", he replied packing her stuff for her.

"Not people like you," she said. He just smiled.

"What does it say?" the question popped again.

Brendan didn't reply.

"Let me see," she walked around the counter to stand beside him and read it.

"French?" she asked. He nodded.

"But now I'm standing beside you, you still want to stand alone?"

"It means I can even if you walk away."

"So then anyone who stands with you isn't important, won't make a difference to you if the person left?" she asked blinking her large eyes.

Brendan ran out of the store. He didn't know where to find her. The airlines won't give any information. So he took the gamble, booked a flight along the same route he met her last and waited.

"You would like something to drink, Sir?" the air hostess asked. He looked at her and sighed.

"I would like to talk to you."

After the flight landed, she approached him.

"What now?" she demanded. He had come this far but he didn't know where to go from here.

"You misinterpreted me," He said.

"About?"

"About this," He pointed at his tattoo.

"No I didn't." she replied with a smile. "You just took too long to interpret my running away". He didn't understand her, the fact that she was smiling didn't help either.

She walked around the table to his side and raised his cuffs to read the tattoo again and then walked the way back picked her purse from the table and was about to leave.

"Wait", he called after her.

"Finally" she exclaimed.

Facing Reality

Maybe it was the nothingness induced by retirement, or maybe the thoughts were triggered the day Mr. Seth's grand-daughter asked him about it in all the innocence attributed to a six year old. The questions brought back a multitude of memories. It was not that the memories were bad, it was just that they were too good and made Mr. Seth sad when he thought about them.

"Grandpa, why is it that you and grandma are never together?" the six year old had asked him one fine day during her summer vacations.

"It's because she has her own set of chores and I've mine," he replied.

That didn't quite satisfy her curiosity. She continued looking at him with her doe-shaped eyes full of curiosity.

"Come here", Mr. Seth said and placed her fragile form on his lap. It was an invitation for her and she revived her quest with renewed vigour. What followed was a plethora of questions, framed in the brutal honesty of her age and inexperience.

"My parents share their room, you don't, why?"

"I never see you and grandma sharing a meal together"

"You and grandma never sit for hours and chitchat; we sit for hours together and talk in our home."

The questions went on and on, after a time Mr. Seth had a hard time answering all her queries.

"Is it because you both have been together for so long that you have run out of things to say to each other?" She finally concluded when she couldn't extract any satisfactory information from Mr. Seth.

They had been together for 30 long years, and if he could remember correctly they had run out of things to say to each other in the fourth year of their marriage itself. When all the pretenses were done with, there was nothing left to prove to each other, the romanticism of the youth had withered away, boredom had crept in along with the practicality of everyday life and what was left was an ordinary life where Mr. Seth was the bread-winner and Mrs. Seth was the household help.

The only thing that added spice to their life was the constant bickering of Mrs. Seth. She had finally realized the grave mistake she had committed in committing her life to Mr. Seth. Leaving the elite of her parents' house and eloping with Mr. Seth had been the biggest mistake of her life as she put it. She made it a point to make Mr. Seth realize the sacrifices she had made to be his wife. And Mr. Seth usually went in his own shell when she was in such a mood.

Mr. Seth was never a great conversationalist. He had just donned that hat when he was courting Mrs. Seth. They belonged to different strata of the society, yet he had made every effort to win her over. He had successfully masked his lack of intelligence by being quiet most of the times. Mrs. Seth interpreted it as his gentleman's attitude, where he allowed her to do most of the talking, always dined in her favourite restaurant and other little things like that which made Mrs. Seth think that he was considerate towards her when in reality he was just ignorant.

Mr. Seth remembered with fondness the idealism of his youth when he was a free bird. He was never overly concerned about his place in society. His idea of a happy life was restricted to good food and bare necessities of life. He never cared for the luxuries. He had almost always believed in doing things just because they had to be done. He lacked the ambition that people around him had to scale the heights in their professional life. He didn't have anything he was overly passionate about. In fact, for most of the time he was just happy being alive. Then gradually his friends started getting married and he knew he had to.

His hunt for a perfect bride had resulted in many escapades in his youth. The incidents he remembered with a sigh now. He had met his future wife through his friends and decided to pursue her for a while. There were no promises made, but Mr. Seth had somehow underestimated his charms. He didn't realize that Mrs. Seth was impressed by him and she had decided to marry him against all odds. It was only on her insistence that he managed to run away with her against the will of her family. He had not given it much of a thought then and eloped only because Mrs. Seth said that they have to. There was no other way out.

Mr. Seth had never conveyed his undying love, never promised the stars for her but she had somehow heard it all without him saying so. His friends praised him for his valor and he started believing that he was born just for this cause. Initially he tried to be the person, Mrs. Seth thought him to be but it started to wear him off and then the squabbling started.

Mrs. Seth never gave in her efforts to make Mr. Seth the person she believed he was before they married. She somehow started believing that the reason for his changed attitude lied in her. Subconsciously, she adapted his way of life but in reality she still strived for the high standards. She would wait for Mr. Seth to return from his meagre job, and the moment he arrived she would start narrating her day right from the time she got up, because the neighbours were too loud to every single detail of the things that went wrong the whole day through only because she married the wrong man.

The outside world saw them as the perfect couple with the quiet demeanor of Mr. Seth and the interesting presence of Mrs. Seth. The wives of Mr. Seth's colleagues envied Mrs. Seth because she had the independence of running her home her way. Mr. Seth never interfered in any of her work.

With the passage of time, Mrs. Seth got new reasons to complain about her life when her children arrived. The kids always saw their mother as their source of inspiration. Mr. Seth was around but never there for them. He had started spending more and more time with himself and Mrs. Seth had found solace in her kids. They were her new hope in life. Her only way to escape from the wretched life she was living for past many years.

Mr. Seth had nothing to complain. He always found his food at the dining table on time; all his clothes were always ironed and immaculately kept in his cupboard. He was complacent with his way of life. His children never placed any demands on him. All his communication with them was through his wife. Mrs. Seth would decide when the demands of her children exceeded Mr. Seth's limits. At times like this, she would strive to fulfil her children's wishes by herself through her savings. But she never bothered Mr. Seth. She had quietly accepted his shortcomings.

When their children grew up, got married and had their own kids, Mr. Seth was always a distant figure for his grand kids. They somehow preferred Mrs. Seth's company.

It was only when, their younger daughter gave birth to a girl-child that Mr. Seth became involved with her. It was the remark from Mr. Seth's son-in-law that made him take notice. His son-in-law commented that the newborn resembled Mr. Seth, right from her doe shaped eyes to the cleft in her chin. Mrs. Seth refused to accept the similarity. "She is so small, let's see how she turns out when she is few days older," she said.

In fact, she grew up to resemble Mr. Seth not only in looks but in her character too. She preferred her own company and was always too busy in her own world in spite of repeated efforts of her parents to make her more outgoing. She would visit her grandparents in her vacations and spend hours in her grandfather's room, where Mr. Seth would sit reading and she would just be near him playing with her dolls or seeing the pictures in the books.

Initially, Mr. Seth had a hard time accepting the attachment that the kid was showing towards him, but then he started buying comics and bringing chocolates for her. It was the closest anyone had ever seen Mr. Seth get to anyone. Gradually their bond grew stronger and Mr. Seth found himself narrating funny stories from his childhood to her. It was then that the child asked Mr. Seth about his relationship with her grandmother.

Mr. Seth spent that night in retrospection. He remembered the time he had exaggerated everything about himself in a hope to please Mrs. Seth at his friends' party, where he met her for the first time. He recalled the endless meetings at various coffee houses or other places of Mrs. Seth's choice when he would spend hours listening to her talks. He remembered the parties after their marriage, where Mrs. Seth would be at her best and nearly everyone would congratulate him on finding such a beautiful and intelligent wife. He would beam with pride but never say anything to Mrs. Seth. She almost always had some not-so-good things to say about the people who had just hours ago praised her in Mr. Seth's presence upon returning home. He had a hard time remembering anything else, because that were the last happy memories he carried of her. He suddenly started regretting not knowing anything about her now.

The next morning he found the newspaper with his breakfast at the dining table. He could hear Mrs. Seth in the kitchen. He couldn't recall the last time he had disturbed her for anything he needed. If Mrs. Seth forgot to put something he needed, which she seldom did, he would fetch it himself without calling her. He did that now too, but saw Mrs. Seth with the corner of his eye. She was busy doing something, she always was.

That afternoon he joined the family for lunch, something he never had done for past many years. His grand-daughter was at his side and seemed very happy to see Mr. Seth at the dining table. The rest of the family was surprised but concealed it really well. On other days, Mr. Seth could hear laughter at the table, as the family dined and he spent time in his study. But that day everyone was quiet.

"Grandpa, How did you meet grandma?" his grand-daughter asked him.

Everyone stopped eating, and hands were in mid air, as Mr. Seth's grand-daughter continued looking at him for an answer and her parents continued looking at the child with anger. Mrs. Seth never looked up from the plate.

"It's a long story," Mr. Seth replied and then he narrated the whole episode of their first meeting, he stole glances at

Mrs. Seth for any reaction and she gave none. He was honest in his narration and his words enunciated his fondness for Mrs. Seth, something he had never vocalized before.

He was at the point in his narration, where he had mustered the courage to ask Mrs. Seth out for lunch when his daughter interrupted, "But was it allowed back then?" Her question was directed at no one in particular, because she had almost never asked Mr. Seth anything in her life.

"It wasn't" Mr. Seth replied. "At least not in my part of the world, but then I could not let that come in between, I was totally bowled over by her" he added with a wink at his daughter. She could have fallen off her chair at his gesture, she was that surprised.

"I heard you two eloped?" his son-in-law asked.

What followed was another past reminisce from Mr. Seth with all the twists and turns and exaggerations that can be attributed only to a master story teller. His grand-daughter was jubilant, nearly everyone at the table had tears in their eyes, Mr. Seth made them laugh that much. Only Mrs. Seth remained quiet.

"But then I lost track of things". Mr. Seth continued looking at his wife. "In the exhilaration of my youth I had managed to win over a girl I could only hope to in my dreams. And when my dreams turned to reality, I had no idea how to deal with it." He looked at Mrs. Seth again but she never looked up.

"Your mother has had a tough time living with me," he continued looking at his daughter. "She had coped with everything while I remained a silent spectator," he concluded.

That evening the whole family went out to the garden on the insistence of Mr. Seth's grand-daughter. She was in high spirits to see all the people she loved around, her parents and grandparents. Mr. and Mrs. Seth sat on the bench watching her play with her parents. It was after many years that they had shared such an intimacy.

Mr. Seth had dinner with his family again. They all laughed over anecdotes Mr. Seth narrated even as Mrs. Seth maintained a dignified silence. After dinner, almost unconsciously, Mr. Seth went to Mrs. Seth's room. A place they had not shared for about 15 years. She didn't complain.

Mrs. Seth quietly passed away in her sleep that night.

Living with Shadows

The way he walked always stood out. Sheekha could've recognized him from miles away. This time around she knew she had to somehow camouflage herself so that he won't notice her. She lowered her head, wrapped her shawl closely around her and took fast hurried steps in a hope to diminish her already tiny frame and be out of his eye as fast as possible.

Yugaant didn't miss her. There were about a hundred people walking on the pavement and he had this weird habit of mentally drawing a graph of everything. This time it was of the bars generated by the varying heights of people walking towards him. Presently, he was doing that again, most of the people he was facing were of the same height, so his bar chart was pretty uniform and then there was a steep drop. She was the reason for the graph to drop suddenly. That's when he saw her. He also saw her efforts to ignore him. That made him smile.

As she passed him, he called after her. For a moment Sheekha thought of paying no attention. But almost unconsciously she stopped and turned.

"It's been a long time. How are you?" he asked.

Sheekha recalled the last time they had met in the hospital, when she was a total emotional wreck and he had taken care of everything for her.

She smiled. He was in front of her in two long strides. "How are you?" he asked again.

She didn't answer, just smiled. Sheekha looked up to him. He was smiling. The way old friends grin when they meet someone after a long gap. Who was she kidding? He wasn't her friend. At one time he was her colleague and then he was her employer, but her friend? She had never seen him as a friend.

"Care to walk?" He asked her. Almost instantly, he took her hand, even before she nodded in yes. They passed the crowded streets to the quiet lanes lit by lamps at fixed distances so that they gave birth to shadows that grew at a monstrous rate scaring Sheekha as they took a huge form in front of her and then died again to be reborn even before she could scream. All of it occurred at a rhythmic pace, and Sheekha lived the different chapters her life was divided in, in every birth and death of their shadows.

Yugaant noticed the shadows too, but for him it symbolized them. The birth signified the day he met her for the first time at the office building, a girl who seldom looked away from her computer screen. The growth of her shadow made him remember the time he had seen her transform from the shy girl he thought she was to be the fun loving person he met just hours later at the office party thrown to welcome new joiners. She had almost stolen the whole show by winning all the competitions right from the infamous GK quiz that comprised of just silly questions to test the sense of humour of the new stock in the company. She had even found a mistake in one of the fun questions. The everyday office joker who had arranged the whole quiz was pretty offended by it, but deep down everyone knew he had competition now.

Yugaant was the judge to the skit competition organized for them; he was totally bowled over by the funny lines and the relevance of the act her group had put up. He had to ask them who wrote it all at the end of it and all fingers pointed at her. After winning about four of such events, she went silent. Yugaant found her sitting alone in a corner and joined her.

"Tired?" He had asked her then.

She gave a weak smile, and nodded. Yugaant had spent about an hour talking to her, and she didn't sound fun as if the spell had worn off. She was again the quiet person; he had thought her to be. After that she had shown just glimpses of that fun-loving personality, but preferred to be quiet for most of the day. She was the best at her work but never socialized. She rejected every offer to be the part of any club in the office.

You couldn't exactly point a finger at it, but something was wrong with her and Yugaant knew it, still she intrigued him, he had seen a side of Sheekha that refused to go away. He invited her to parties, and she religiously refused, or promised to come and didn't show up and Yugaant never gave up.

Yugaant met her one day on the way to office, she was walking the way she did with fast hurried steps, he offered her a lift, Sheekha's eyes refused, but then she accepted on impulse.

"So you stay alone in this city?" he asked her as she hopped on his bike.

"Yeah."

"Where's your family?" Yugaant asked her just to carry forward the conversation.

"I guess you have access to my file in HR", Sheekha replied.

Yugaant was shocked. She was being rude and he had not expected it.

"Yeah, but it's easier this way," he smiled back. It was Sheekha's turn to be surprised.

Yugaant never again met her on the way to office. He either found her already there in the office when he reached or she came in late. He tried to convince himself that it was a coincidence, but he knew it wasn't, she was avoiding him.

He saw her again on a weekend in a mall, with a group of friends; she seemed to have a great time. What was it with this girl? She was almost the same girl at the office event the first day. Yugaant took a table near her where he could see her, but not she. Hell, she won't have seen him, even if he sat right next to her she was that preoccupied. Yugaant saw Sheekha placing a bet on winning a round of pool with her friends, he was stuck to his seat when she did win the bet, then went on to dare a stranger on the pool table and win that bet too as her friends applauded. She even sang at the live karaoke amidst loud claps from her friends. Sheekha excused herself after that and vanished in the girls' room. Yugaant decided on leaving, he had somehow concluded that she was happy in her own world and didn't want new friends. He was provoked by the thought. She was an impostor to him now, who wore mask to work, who was a shrewd woman. His eyes blazed with anger as he pushed his chair back and got up to leave. But then he saw her sneak past her group of friends to the balcony. Almost instantly, Yugaant followed. Probably, it was that sad look on her face, or maybe he saw tear stains that made him go after her.

It was pretty dark in the balcony. He couldn't see her, but then he saw a tip of a burning cigarette and saw her behind it. She didn't make a happy scene, it was like seeing an overworked clown from circus after the curtain falls down, and the paint wears off. Yugaant felt a pang of sympathy towards her; she was turning into a puzzle he so desperately wanted to solve.

They didn't talk in the week that followed, but Yugaant kept a close watch on her. He was almost stalking her. She knew he was but it didn't matter to her. For her, he didn't exist. The turning point in their relationship was when an overworked colleague at work got provoked by something which wasn't exactly Sheekha's fault, but he misunderstood that it was and started a verbal assault at her. It was probably the first time that someone was subjecting her to such a treatment and Sheekha went numb. She wanted to cry as he went on shouting but she couldn't, she was just glued to her place and not a word came out of her mouth. It was then that Yugaant came to her rescue. Being a senior, he had put that irate colleague in place.

"There", he said once that person was pacified and back at his desk. Sheekha still wasn't in a state to react. She was as silent as a statue. "You're fine?" Yugaant asked. But she didn't reply. Her eyes had grown wide and she was shaking. Yugaant pulled a chair for her and repeated the question.

"That bastard". Sheekha said after a while. Yugaant couldn't help but smile.

"Alright, we don't exactly need the sobriquets here." He smiled. "You're still shaking", he added.

"I know", Sheekha replied. "I need to get out of this crappy place".

"Another superlative, anyway I'll come with you."

"No", Sheekha objected, and ran out of the rows of cubicles to the open space. Yugaant followed anyway.

"Why the hell are you stalking me?" Sheekha yelled once they reached the room officially termed as the "smoking zone".

"You know, it's not a great idea to yell at your boss" Yugaant replied closing the heavy wooden door. "Bad impression, I carry a reputation", he added.

Sheekha was speechless. Usually when she wanted to get at a distance from someone, rudeness worked but it wasn't working with this man.

"What do you want from me?" she asked him.

Yugaant just shrugged.

"Can't you just leave me alone?" she asked after sometime in which Yugaant kept looking at her and she kept ignoring him.

"Disgusting!" She exclaimed when Yugaant showed no signs of getting out of the room and walked past him.

"I was there once", Yugaant said after her and she stopped.

"You were where?" she questioned.

"You know where", he replied. Suddenly he was at loss for words. He had started it but had no idea what he wanted to say and she was standing with hands on her hips waiting for him to continue.

"Where you are right now." He offered as a means of explanation.

"Where am I?" Sheekha asked exasperated.

"Nothing just go", he replied and damned himself a thousand times for coming so close and blowing it up. He had for a second seen her guard fall down but he was too late.

The next few weeks, Yugaant spent in finding anything and everything he could about her. He knew it was insane but he felt this terrible urge to find everything about her. He even called for that file in HR. Sheekha came from a well-to-do family, seemed to have scored excellent grades in college and extra-curricular. She had some great references too. But then why was she so strange, it amazed him.

A month later another incident in office, showed Sheekha throwing her papers in. It so happened that they had there annual review which was taken by Yugaant's boss. That person had the reputation of being a total jerk. Sheekha was called in for the review, where Yugaant being her immediate boss and his boss faced her. She was asked some general questions about her performance and what her future plans with the company were.

But then the boss carried it a bit too far and asked her about her personal plans. Sheekha shrank back a bit, but he carried on.

"What are your long-term plans?" he asked.

"I already told you." Sheekha replied.

"Yeah, yeah, I know. I can read it here," "you plan to learn the latest software in market, see yourself two positions up, that puts this young man's job in danger", he continued reading from the sheet Sheekha had filled in, while putting a hand on Yugaant's shoulder at the mention of his name.

"That's pretty much it then," Sheekha replied.

"What I mean…" he continued with a stupid grin "…is with your life. You will get married and stuff right; you need to plan that too."

"And how does that bother you?" Sheekha asked totally offended.

"You need to" he continued. "What are you 24" he added?

"And who are you? My dad?" Sheekha refuted.

Yugaant knew he should have interrupted much earlier. Things were getting out of hand. He knew how impulsive Sheekha was. Before he could react, Sheekha was out of the room, the door was still swinging after her hasty exit. His boss was stunned. In a way he was too.

Sheekha never returned to the office. She sent in her resignation through the only colleague she was at a more than professional relation with.

Looking back, Yugaant couldn't find the reason for her leaving; she could've handled the whole thing differently and not have made a big deal out of it. But she being the way she was, Yugaant couldn't expect anything else. He wanted to forget her as an insane co-worker, but he couldn't.

He always found out about her through that colleague. From what he heard she was doing well. A year later when Yugaant left his job to start his own firm, he gave an advertisement in the newspapers and requested the colleague Sheekha who was still in touch with to make sure she saw it.

Sheekha saw the ad, came in for the interview and was selected. She was always good at her work, in fact, the best, Yugaant tried to reason himself for his actions.

It had been a year but she was pretty much the same.

Around Christmas, Yugaant announced a Christmas party and to make sure she attends, he announced that he would inform everyone about promotions and raises in the party. Something he had the liberty of doing now that he was in-charge. Sheekha did come and soon lost herself in all the events organized. Yugaant kept an eye on her throughout and she looked happy. She was laughing, talking to everyone, trying her hand at every game from darts to pool. It was nice to see her like that, but Yugaant knew that would pass. And as he predicted about an hour later, just before the dinner, he saw her collecting her purse, about to leave.

Yugaant made his way across the room.

"Why are you leaving?" he asked once he reached her.

"I need to get home, it's late." She replied without looking up at him.

"Yeah, but have dinner and then I'm going to announce the promotions, you don't want to miss that?" he said to make her stay.

"I just joined, Yugaant, I am not getting anything. What's the point?" She asked

"You will get dinner." Yugaant replied. He knew it was a terrible excuse but hoped it would work.

She smiled and stayed.

"Level 1—Cleared" Yugaant thought.

Yugaant was doing all he could possibly do to understand her, he even surfed the internet in hope of finding a psychological condition to explain her behaviour, nothing fitted the bill. How can a person be so different within hours? The thought never left him. Sheekha did.

Almost suddenly, Sheekha stopped coming to work, this time the resignation came in through mail. Yugaant was shocked. He replied that she had to come meet him for clearing the dues. She replied back that she was going out of town so she couldn't. Yugaant finally gave up.

Next time he saw her was after a fortnight of her resignation. She had lied. She was very much in town. Yugaant saw her in the same mall he had seen her earlier, this time with a man of about 50. They looked deeply in discussion; maybe the man was in the process of explaining something to Sheekha, because she kept nodding a lot. It was the most Yugaant could make out from the distance.

It was stupid and totally insane but Yugaant followed the man after he had said his byes to Sheekha and he did enter a hospital. A million thoughts ran through his mind, was she on dope? Is she really insane? He couldn't make anything out of it. He followed that man as he entered his room, the glass plate outside his room read:

Dr. K.S. Rao

M.D. Psychiatrist & Counselor.

She really had a problem. It scared him. Still he entered the room.

"You have an appointment?" the doctor asked him.

"I don't, but can you just spare a few minutes, I need to ask something," Yugaant replied.

The doctor looked at him for a while and then asked him to take a seat.

"It's my lunch time", he said.

"I'm really sorry doctor but I won't be long", Yugaant expressed his apologies and then added,

"It's about the girl you were with in the mall."

The doctor gave him a stern look. "I don't discuss my patients".

"Patients!" The word registered in his mind and Yugaant continued his quest.

"I understand that, but you see I'm really worried about her. I used to work with her and then she abruptly left." He tried to explain himself as best as he could. He knew he could be thrown out any second, but it didn't matter.

"If I'm not wrong, you are Mr. Yugaant?" the doctor asked him.

"You know me?" Yugaant was surprised.

"I'm also her counselor and I must say your name has come out many times", he took a deep breath. "I'm going out of my way here." He added before shutting up.

"What is wrong with her?" Yugaant asked him.

"Why are you so interested?" the doctor asked him instead of answering his question.

He had no answer. But he knew he somehow had to convince the man he was facing.

"I don't know." He replied honestly. "But somehow I feel I need to help her out, with her parents staying in another town, that's the most human thing I can do." He went on blabbering for a while.

"Have you informed her parents?" he added as an afterthought.

"She doesn't want to inform them", the doctor replied. He spent the next few minutes well beyond his stipulated lunch time to explain Yugaant her condition, the causes and the implications.

"I initially termed it as mood swings, but lately she has shown signs of a deeper ailing." The doctor explained. "I wanted to call her parents, but she is an adult and totally opposes the idea." He went on "I had it under control, but certain pressures on her have pushed it too far. I have to take her in." He concluded.

"Take her in?" Yugaant asked again.

"She has become psychotic. Loosing sense of reality, I have to admit her before she causes any danger to herself," the doctor went on explaining in pure clinical terms.

Yugaant was in a state of disbelief. What if she was okay and this doctor was driving her crazy? Why did she even take such a huge step and go to see a psychiatrist. Many questions raised through his mind.

"We can't help her you mean?" Yugaant asked.

"It's beyond that", the doctor explained. "I know it's hard to accept that's why she doesn't want to inform her parents. But problems do exist and turning a blind eye to it is not going to solve it. We have a social stigma attached to everything around here right from migraine to something more serious. Instead of ignoring it, a proper treatment is essential; in her case she is going to be fine."

The doctor's words kept ringing in his head as Yugaant walked his way back home.

(ii)

They continued walking in that lane, each of them speechless. Yugaant still had a thousand things to say to her and Sheekha was too embarrassed to even look up at him. She had not informed him about her discharge from the hospital but had instead decided to be on her own for a while. Somehow Yugaant never seemed to get out of her life.

She relived the moments in the hospital where out of nowhere Yugaant had come to see her.

She was living in the private clinic of Dr. Rao where her room consisted of just a bed and chair, the doctor said she was improving, she was far from it. And then one day she had got deep into suicidal ideation. It was the day Yugaant had come to see her. The moment she saw him, she got irritated.

"What are you doing here?" Sheekha almost yelled at him. Yugaant didn't reply.

"I want you out of here", she shouted again and Yugaant turned up to go. But then she stopped him.

"You know where I live?" She asked him. Yugaant nodded.

"Good !" she continued, "I have a car and there is some stuff up in my apartment, I want you to take it."

"What for?" Yugaant asked.

"Just like that. I won't need it." Sheekha concluded.

"You would", Yugaant replied. "And yeah once you come out of here, I really want to drive that car of yours." He smiled.

"What did you mean that day when you said that you have been where I am?" Sheekha asked him. Her thoughts were racing ahead of her and he was having a hard time keeping up the pace.

Yugaant took a while before replying as if he was putting his thoughts together.

"I've been through this when I was younger, in fact, younger than you and there was no one to stand by me. I survived it alone. I just want you to know that I will stand by you no matter what." He said and came out of the room. Dr. Rao was waiting for him there.

"You've been through this?" the doctor asked him.

"You heard all that?" Yugaant was surprised.

"All the rooms are watched." He replied. "The risks involved are substantial. But that doesn't answer my question." He continued looking at him for an answer.

"I lied". Yugaant replied. "I couldn't make her believe any other way that everything will be fine without example."

Dr. Rao smiled in agreement.

The next time their shadows took the grotesque form, Sheekha actually got scared and clutched his hand.

"What?" he asked.

"Nothing", she replied leaving his hand.

"The shadows", Yugaant replied for her. "It's strange."

"What is?" Sheekha asked.

"The shadows. They never leave you. They keep dancing around you a bit too loud in sunlight, and then keep a lingering presence in moonlight. But always there. Our constant companion", he remarked.

"Not true," Sheekha replied. "They leave us in our darkest hours." She said looking up at him. All the years he had just been there stood before her eyes.

In the coming years, Yugaant never told her that he had lied to her in the hospital and he never told Dr. Rao that the lie wasn't totally a lie. He had in fact survived it all with her.

Achilles' Heel

It was her theatrical debut, a childhood dream finally turning into reality. The day had been a part of countless pleasant reveries. Rhea wanted to live in a world where you could be a different someone almost everyday, enacting the life of a perfect stranger and in the process being that person, when you offered a part of yourself to that character and a much larger part of that character's persona became you. When sometimes you brought to life a larger than life character forever sculptured by history, would giving birth feel any different? She had participated in many a plays during her schooling, but this opportunity was huge. She was going to star into an experimental musical directed by the most famous playwright of the day. All her hard work, the innumerable rehearsals, voice training and staying away from everything that could cause harm to her voice had paid off. She was playing the lead, a role till date she could only fantasize about.

Rhea was "Miya" a young girl from the early nineties who loses her husband in a war and the story of Miya picks up from the point where she gets the news of his demise, wherein she had to perform a solo expressing her sorrow. Rhea's understanding of music had landed her the role in the first place, or so she thought. Rhea was selected in the audition from about fifteen girls; she had outdone everyone including a strong contender, Anusha, who was rumored to be the director's muse. The musical progressed further where Miya dreams that her husband is alive in the hills and so begins her odyssey where she meets various characters. Finally, Miya lands up in the hills and meets her husband who is now happily married to a local, older woman, Chhaya. Miya realizes that her husband doesn't remember her. She convinces Chhaya, who gives her a chance to make her husband recall her existence. Miya fails, as her husband still doesn't recognize her. What follows is Miya's struggle to win him back. Chhaya, at the same time feels that Miya is ruining her life and suggests that one of them had to die as they loved the same man and couldn't possibly live their life longing, one of them had to give up and as destiny favored her, the one to die has to be Miya. The play climaxes with Miya's death in a duel with Chhaya where an extremely provoked Chhaya kills her. As Miya takes her final breath, she sees a flash of recognition in her husband's eyes and she dies with a peaceful smile on her face.

Anusha was selected to play Chhaya. She had been the female protagonist in many productions but this musical was Miya's story while she was reduced to a secondary character. After the audition, the director had arranged a story-telling session to elucidate his vision to the entire cast. They were seated in a circle with the director standing at the centre. His narration had brought life to each and every character, he laughed with Miya and her husband in their happy days, his voice broke with emotion as he read the lyrics of Miya's solo song, words which displayed her longing. He spoke with a different kind of authority which fell short of rudeness and went ahead of being courteous when he became Chhaya and at the end, with Miya's death, his voice shed tears while his eyes didn't. Rhea knew that she was in love then and there.

The rehearsals had begun almost three months before the scheduled opening. The director wanted every member of his troupe to share his passion. He had an innate obsession with the play. The members of the troupe and the backstage crew called him Mr. Lunatic in his absence and almost everyone called him "Joe" lovingly. They started with the opening sequence where Rhea had to express deep grief on the news of her husband's death and perform a solo to convey her distress; Rhea was nineteen and had led a happy, content life, grief for her meant breaking a fingernail. She was unable to bring the sentiment Joe wanted out of her. He lost his patience and summoned Anusha to guide her. Rhea somehow took an instant dislike for Anusha. Rhea had a quality that everyone liked her and she had developed the tendency of being distinctly polite to everyone even if she didn't feel an instantaneous fondness for that person. But with Anusha it was different. One look at her and an inner voice said, "I hate you". Rhea tried to shrug it off. But even as Anusha went on explaining the depth of the scene and what was expected of her, the inner voice refused to be quiet. Rhea couldn't make out why that happened, she couldn't be indifferent to her, and she couldn't let it go. She just had to hate her. Anusha was everything that Rhea was not. She had poise; attitude and a straight deep voice hoarsened by smoke that gave her an influential aura. Anusha was not charming, she wasn't the conventional beauty but she gave the impression of exquisiteness, everything about her was magnificent. When she entered the theatre, the big room shrank around her; she walked with a panache which lessened everything and everyone around her. And when she spoke, the other person was forced to rethink his existence; her manner conveyed that she didn't care what anyone thinks or does.

Her eyes held an expression of inexorable calm but one read the tense vitality in them, the raging blaze which made one think that she was at war with the world.

Anusha had played the "Helen of Troy" in her last theatre appearance. When Rhea read in the papers that Anusha was to play that part, she had held the paper with Anusha's picture on it and her first thought was, "she isn't that beautiful" but that was before Rhea met her. Now as Anusha was in the same room as her, Rhea couldn't think of a better person to have successfully portrayed that character. Anusha wasn't just a face that could launch a thousand ships, she was one who could instigate desperate persuasion and annihilation by her disappearance and that was why Rhea hated her.

Rhea on the other hand could just be described in one word–cute.

"Miya symbolizes purity," Joe explained in the next group session he took after each day's practice to bring everyone closer to the play. "You complement Chhaya," he continued focusing totally on Rhea. His blue-grey eyes pierced into Rhea's skin as he went on, "Miya is an epitome of everything fresh, innocent and untouched, she has just one aim in life, that of pure love, she is obsessed with finding her only true love, she knows nothing else except the fact that she has to be with that one person, she lives for it and finally dies for it." He concluded.

"And how do you see Chhaya, Joe?" Anusha questioned.

Joe's shifted his attention from Rhea to the voice that asked him that. Rhea felt like something which was hers was lost. Joe's expression changed as he looked at Anusha for a long time. He had softness in his eyes when he looked at Rhea, the way a shepherd looks at the new born of his sheep. The eyes went a darker, deeper shade of grey as they turned towards Anusha, as if they held a secret in them known only to them and the person they focused on. Anusha held his gaze for a while and they communicated in their own language unknown to everyone who surrounded them and with absolute disregard to audience presence.

"How do you see Chhaya, Anush?" he asked Anusha instead after the pause.

The shortening of name made Rhea wince, it made her realize that they two indeed shared a relationship which was alien to her. She almost instantly made her mind to reach that point where she would be seen as a part of them and not as an outsider. The thoughts made her lose most part of Anusha's answer, when she jolted to reality she heard Anusha say, "... Chhaya is real, she doesn't live in a fantasy world, she knows what belongs to her is hers." The man who played her husband in the play interrupted at this point with his part of argument.

"But that doesn't give her the right to murder Miya, she was cruel," he argued.

Anusha just laughed the way one laughs when confronted with the ignorance of the unintelligent. Rhea looked at Joe, but he had eyes just for Anusha as she countered.

"She is cruel, just because she knows what she wants?"

"Doesn't justify." The man argued again.

"What would you do if someone acts smart with your wife?" Anusha asked the man, looking straight at him. The calm refused to part ways with her eyes, even as she disagreed with him.

"Kill him". The man replied brutally as if in a second he had visualized the whole episode and was actually wringing the neck of the hypothetical person.

"That's what Chhaya did." Anusha replied placidly.

"And that's why you're playing Chhaya." Joe exclaimed almost instantly. He was happy with his decision or so it seemed.

"She was taking advantage of an unstable man." Rhea said.

Everyone looked at her, some with approval and some blankly while the rest looked at Joe for his answer.

"That's great, Rhea, continue hating her that would add spice to your character", Joe laughed and the session was dismissed.

"But she did", Rhea said to herself as everyone left the studio.

The next day went with Rhea rehearsing her solo. There were very few people in the studio as the day was scheduled for Rhea's song.

"At a higher octave", Joe instructed as Rhea sang.

"Don't just sing it, feel the words." He shouted next. Rhea went silent. She just stared at him.

"I know it's difficult but try", Joe added in a lower voice.

Rhea sang the same words many a times, her throat had started to ache, but Joe still felt that something was amiss.

"I will sing it as it should be in the recording, Joe", Rhea said finally giving up. She just couldn't match his standards.

"What recording?" Joe questioned. And then laughed as he understood what Rhea meant.

"There's no recording, dear, everything is L-I-V-E," he enunciated for affect.

Rhea's eyes went wider as realization struck her. Joe was laughing as Rhea started panicking.

"You mean I have to sing it out on stage?" she asked, almost yelling. Joe just nodded.

"Out there?"

Joe nodded again.

"Why else do you think I selected you?" He added.

Rhea was shaking now.

"I can't do it", she said at last.

"You can", Joe countered and then he announced a much awaited break which he utilized in trying to pacify Rhea.

They ordered lunch and Joe watched with fascination as Rhea ate her boiled vegetables and bland stuff she called food.

"How can you?" he asked.

"Why else do you think you selected me?" Rhea laughed chewing on a cucumber.

Joe laughed too. Rhea continued looking at Joe as he turned the pages of the printed script with one hand and ate his food with the other. His dedication amazed her. She had heard his name some years back for the first time as the play he had directed and starred in won accolades at various levels. Rhea had seen that play as a fifteen year old and she could say, in a way that it was influential in her decision to enter the field. She remembered watching Joe on stage in that play. He seemed so much at ease. Rhea had eyes just for him.

"You don't act anymore?" Rhea asked all of a sudden.

"Let's say, I am content in direction", Joe replied without looking up.

"I saw your last play as an actor." Rhea said again.

Joe didn't reply and Rhea guessed that she had walked into no-man's land. She mentally listed all the plays he had acted in or directed and then she realized that Anusha was a part of his every play. The realization hurt her.

"You have any specific ideas for the climax?" Joe suddenly asked her and then without waiting for her answer he continued, "You know a song sounds great, but I am confused now, maybe a war of words would be better." He concluded for himself. "Maybe I will ask Anusha when she comes in tomorrow." He added.

Rhea had to reply now. "I can pull off a song." She replied.

"I know you can, why else you think I selected you?" Joe winked at her.

Anusha walked in the next day to rehearse her scenes with Rhea. She wasn't a tall woman, almost the same height as Rhea but somehow Rhea felt like she always looked up to her. Her personality demanded that. She almost made Rhea cry when Rhea couldn't get her lines straight.

"This is useless, what are we dealing with here, some ill rehearsed street play?" Anusha exclaimed even as tears filled Rhea's eyes.

Joe interrupted and pacified Anusha. She took a break and Joe came to Rhea who was still sobbing. Rhea expected some kind of solace from his presence.

"You need extra practice, girl", he said. His absolute lack of sympathy shocked her but she nodded.

The backstage crew acted with more compassion.

"Grow up fast girl," they instructed her, "we don't call her the iron-lady for no reason".

"She is rude", Rhea complained.

"She is the best, and she expects the best from everyone, understand that." The oldest person from the crew called "dada" by everyone remarked. He was a compassionate man who single-handedly managed the lights and sound effects during the play. He had given 25 years to the stage and his old eyes outlined with wrinkles always held an expression of kindness. Dada entertained everyone with his anecdotes from the past during the breaks. He had seen a decade change in the theatre and his stories held his experience.

"Doesn't justify", the man who played Rhea's husband argued. "She has to understand that it's Rhea's debut, she on the other hand has loads of experience behind her," he added.

"I've seen Anusha's first play, *beta*," Dada continued, "she was outstanding, her act had the maturity which seasoned actors gain only after years of experience," he concluded.

Now everyone was speechless. No one argued with Dada, his every word was measured. Dada closed doors on every argument with his lash of experience.

Rhea had her lunch with the crew, looking at Joe and Anusha on the other side of the room, having their lunch. They didn't talk much but Rhea heard their conversation loud and clear. There was a deep rooted understanding between them. Rhea watched as Anusha handed Joe his glass of water just as Joe made a movement. She read his mind and Rhea despised that.

Dada watched Rhea as she watched them.

"They go back together a long way", he said.

"I have heard that," Rhea replied.

"Once upon a time, they were going to get married. But then something happened." He informed her.

"What happened?" Rhea asked out of curiosity. She knew that Dada always had all the answers.

"Don't know much, in fact no one does but the fact remains that she is his only inspiration." He replied, his manner conveyed the admiration he held for both Joe and Anusha.

Rhea got up at that.

The extra rehearsals arranged for Rhea meant she had to spend more time with Joe, when all the others left.

"You won't be the best unless you give yourself whole heartedly into it." Joe mentioned one day after the rehearsals. They were alone and Rhea was packing for the day.

"I won't lie to you Joe, theatre is just a hobby, and I can't be as dedicated to anything as you are." Rhea replied with a smile. "It simply amazes me", she added.

Her honesty and easy manner had impressed Joe. Whenever he looked at her, he saw her smiling or laughing at some joke with the crew or actually cracking that joke. When Rhea was on stage, she showed full interest in her character. What Joe desired was devotion but he was ready to trade her jubilant presence with her feeble effort to become Miya.

"You believe that life shouldn't be taken seriously, right?" Joe asked.

Rhea just nodded and the effortless grin reappeared.

"Doesn't work", Joe replied. He was getting attracted to the simplicity of Rhea's existence but some invisible bonds pulled him back.

"What makes you say that?" Rhea asked. She could almost see Joe's effort to be happy, he laughed with her during the rehearsals, playfully ignored her mistakes but when she looked at him otherwise as he managed certain other things, she saw a cloud of gloom over his head.

"There are three things that make a man—Money, Fame and Power," Joe said. "You don't get either unless you strive for it."

Rhea waited for him to continue but he didn't, as if he had revealed a bit too much and regretted it now.

"You're famous," Rhea counted on her fingers even as Joe looked at her grimly, "your mansion is many people's envy, what else you need to be happy?" Rhea questioned when he refused to speak further.

Joe just shrugged.

"What power?" Rhea asked reading his answer.

"Power to kill," Joe replied and walked away.

Rhea couldn't understand what he meant. Joe never explained.

Things didn't smoothen between Rhea and Anusha. Either one was always mean to the other. Joe never said a word to Anusha and it troubled Rhea. The debate of the climax continued. Rhea was adamant on another song and Anusha felt a confrontation will add depth. Joe was silent.

The only pleasure Rhea derived from the next day's rehearsal was when Joe interrupted Anusha as she said Chhaya's lines. It was short lived but long enough to please Rhea.

"Chhaya represents the enraged love Anush." He explained to her. "Your posture is so composed, it just shows a bit of jealousy, be a bit more aggressive."

"How many real women you know Joe?" Anusha asked him.

Joe smiled. Another unspoken conversation passed between them.

"Trust me, Chhaya is confident and when she has the cards in her favor, why the aggressiveness?" Anusha asked him.

"Calm it is" Joe replied and the conversation was over.

The rehearsals continued. There was so much to do. Dance rehearsals, voice modulation training, songs, sequences, etc. Rhea was the only new comer in the troupe and also the one who needed maximum practice and so the time Rhea spent with Joe increased too. He was a thorough professional. He supported Rhea in every aspect of her character, even when Rhea rehearsed her dance steps with the choreographer, Joe made it a point to be there. He practiced her dialogues with the on-stage husband when the actor who played it left after the day. He listened with the same patience her every take on her solo song.

"That song is the soul of Miya's character; you have to portray her sadness through it, to make people realize how much she needs him in her life," Joe told her.

Rhea practiced that song, she had devised a strategy to demonstrate her distress, the sentiment Joe wanted in the song. Joe was the strategy. Rhea imagined not seeing Joe everyday when the show ended and it tugged at her heart, the feeling translated into her voice as she sung that solo. She finally got it right and even Joe had tears in his eyes.

"You've put life in the song", he exclaimed. That made Rhea's day.

Rhea invited everyone for dinner after the rehearsals that day; it was Anusha's day off so it suited Rhea completely. She was afraid Joe would decline her invitation, but he accepted.

"Only if everyone promises to be on time tomorrow," He said with a grin.

The party was at Rhea's place and continued well in the night. The party had music, great food and drinks, almost everyone got drunk including Joe.

Everyone from the cast was present except Anusha, she was conveniently forgotten. No one mentioned her even once in the party, not even Dada who held a deep-rooted affection for her. Probably everyone knew that Anusha didn't belong to parties, at least not to the kind of party they were having. Even that thought troubled Rhea; she couldn't put her down even after winning the support of everyone around her. Anusha had denied giving Rhea the pleasure of winning against her without saying anything; no matter how high Rhea soared she remained at ground when it came to Anusha.

"But seriously, Joe tell me, Chhaya or Miya?" the man who played Rhea's husband asked in an inebriated state.

"Miya boosts my ego, and Chhaya slashes it down to pieces," Joe replied gesturing to enact the action of a knife cutting through an invisible object that represented his ego.

"So if you were me," the on stage husband continued, "It would be Miya?"

"Definitely, I love Rhea", Joe replied before passing out.

Next day, everyone was back to work with swollen red eyes and a muted silence. The rumors of last night continued though and they reached Anusha, too.

The calmness prevailed.

It was the day when Rhea and Anusha had to rehearse the part where Chhaya suggests that one of them has to die.

Rhea took centre stage as Miya and begged Anusha to give her one chance at meeting her husband.

"*Have mercy and let me see him once, for I come from a long way and only for him.*" Miya sang with deep contempt in her voice as she looked at Anusha.

"*If you must.*" Chhaya replies and a lost looking man who plays their husband entered the stage. He smiles at Chhaya and asks her who Miya is.

Miya pleads with him to remember their good old days but he walks away rejecting her every plea and saying that Chhaya is the only one he knows.

"*You know what's true, just give him away,*

For God is watching the games you play" Miya says to Chhaya.

"*It's very clear that he knows just me,*

You're just a dream he refuses to see" Chhaya replied.

With Anusha's words, Rhea forgot her lines and a smile escaped Anusha's lips. She didn't shout on her, she didn't get irritated like last time. She just laughed.

Joe was provoked, "What is it with you?" he shouted from the front seat of the auditorium where he sat watching them perform.

"Just a week away from the final performance and you don't remember your lines", he exclaimed as he jumped from the seat and was on the stage in few long strides.

"Concentrate on your work not on stupid parties", he added with a scorn in his voice even as his eyes pinned her down. There was a hushed silence as Rhea nodded and picked up her script without any complaints. She was devastated but held her chin up and left the stage.

"You started it." Anusha said to Joe as she walked past him to return to her room.

Joe avoided Rhea for the rest of the day, she was deeply engrossed in getting things right, she knew she had made a fool of herself in front of Anusha and the thought troubled her further. She looked at Joe for comfort but never found him free. Joe was busy with other back stage work; he didn't approach her even once throughout the day. At the end of the day, Rhea waited for him to resume their extra practice. Joe saw her waiting on the stage, as he picked up his bags to return home.

"Go home, Rhea", he said as he opened and closed behind him the door to the theatre. Rhea ran after him, she needed some answers.

"Why are you doing this?" she asked him.

He didn't reply and continued walking towards his car.

"I can tolerate the insults you hurl at me out there", she said motioning at the theatre they left behind "because I know I'm not the best of the actors but I don't deserve this treatment as a human being".

"Just let it be", Joe replied from the rolled down glass window of his car as he seated himself.

"You know what you said yesterday at my party?" she asked.

Joe looked down. He had turned the ignition on but he didn't reply, and Rhea was dead struck on getting an answer out of him. She continued looking at him.

"You want me to make you remember?" she asked with anger.

"I was drunk Rhea not dead, I know every word I said." Joe replied after a long pause. His voice had lost all the weight it carried when he went about giving instructions to everyone.

"Then what did I do to deserve this in just 24 hours?" Rhea asked.

"You are way too young to understand it Rhea, I can just say that I got carried away so just let it be."

"So you mean whatever you said didn't mean a thing?" she asked again.

"I can't lie. I meant everything I said".

"Then what is it?" Rhea asked again.

"It's complicated", Joe replied but at the same time he knew Rhea won't take no for an answer unless she knew the reason too. He gestured her to be in the car.

"We started our career together." He said when Rhea was seated beside him. "I won't be exaggerating if I say that we ruled the stage for a long time. Everyone that time was sure that soon we will be together, but it was all an illusion. If I was good, Anusha was the best. The applause that I assumed to be for us was in reality for her. The audience always clapped a little louder for her. The fame, the recognition, the love was for her, not for me", Joe went on. His eyes held a distant look and Rhea knew that he was reliving his past.

"So that is why you left acting?" Rhea questioned. Joe just nodded.

"I loved her but I didn't want to be with her until I was worthy of her. That's when I shifted completely to writing and direction. I would write a play and offer a minuscule role to her, when she performed the part, her character always became more famous than the main character in the play. I did everything I could, created the most vindictive characters, people would hate but she played the part with such a dignity that people loved her then too, they saw the goodness in her which I never intended as a writer."

"I don't understand you," Rhea exclaimed. Joe smiled. He knew she won't understand because sometimes even he didn't understand what he was doing and for what purpose. He just knew that ten years back, he had started his mission on proving his worth to the only girl he knew then and he still was striving for it.

"When I met you, I realized what being free felt like. I have been so preoccupied with the whole situation that I had forgotten what it felt like to be without any worries. You made me see the wonders in the world, the laughs I had missed during my struggle to be the best. You made me pause and smell the roses around so much so that I just want to run away today from all of this."

"Who is stopping you?" Rhea enquired, she saw a ray of hope. All she wanted to do now was to just be with him, nothing else mattered to her then.

"I have come too far and now I can't turn back, it's just an escape which is very tempting but I can't take it. I have been with her so long that I doubt my existence without her." Joe replied, looking straight at her. There was no regret in his eyes, only a firm ambition. Rhea searched his eyes for any speck of emotion for her but they lacked it. It made her cry and it made her angry at the same time, Rhea suddenly felt cheated when she knew no one had promised her anything, it was only her mind which had woven many fantasies; dreams that were being shattered one by one in front of her now.

"Tempting? Escape?" Rhea laughed. "This is not a damn literary play you're talking about Joe, it's a person, it's Me." She shrieked.

"You won't know how it feels", Joe replied. She didn't. Rhea indeed was too young to understand the cold war, she just knew that having Joe around was comforting and she wanted the comfort to last forever.

"Anusha has the power to murder my self-worth while maintaining her dignity at every step. I lack that power, no matter how hard I try, for her I don't exist. What exists of me is my failure, my pride which she kills with her every successful play, with every applause she gets from the audience. And here I am striving to be the best. From ten years, I just want one moment of victory, a second of watching defeat in her eyes," Joe went on.

Rhea was quiet, she didn't know how to react, the person with her in the car was not the Joe she knew, he just was a shadow of Anusha as she saw him now. It scared her.

"Have you ever seen her eyes, Rhea?" Joe asked her.

Rhea just looked at him. She had no answer. She had seen Anusha's eyes, they were deadpan. Her eyes only came alive when they enacted a scene on stage, otherwise they were void of any emotion and if you looked deeper, you found calm sailing through them.

"You see how calm they are?" Joe asked again. Rhea nodded because she was afraid that if she didn't reply, Joe would shake her up for an answer. He looked hysterical.

"I want the power to kill that calm Rhea", Joe said at last. Rhea got her answer.

(ii)

The grand opening was the next day. Just the mention of the names of two famous people had pulled a crowd to the theatre. It was jam packed.

The show opened with Miya's solo, The crowd burst into applause as Rhea's voice echoed in the theatre.

"A promise I make to myself, each day
To end this bond I'll sure find a way
Never will I remember his existence,
In my solitude, I will find solace,
The name written in the lines of my hand,
Will make it disappear, like a blow on sand,
His memories, I'll kill with hands bare,
For this treasure, I no longer will care,
But whenever I remember the days bygone,
This promise I break every time with a moan.
Let me bask in the love for a little longer,
Let me dream about the past a little longer,
It makes me happy, it makes me stronger.
Let me be the girl of the past, for it's my only armor"

The show progressed and reached the point where Anusha made her entry as Chhaya. Joe noticed people sitting up straighter in the chair.

"It's very clear that he knows just me,
You're just a dream he refuses to see", Chhaya said.

"What will you do, the day he awakens?
When he remembers and me he beckons", Miya asked her.

"I don't see the future, I live in today,
If that day comes, you may take him away."

The scene turns into a melody, where Miya tells Chhaya that she can't live like that any longer, and every hour of separation is slowly killing her.

"Die you must, if that is the case,
For that's the fate you must face", Chhaya replies back.

"This is where you, me differ,
I live so gay and you suffer", she continues. Miya just sobs.

"You can almost feel the tension between them", the on-stage husband remarked as he awaited his entry backstage.

"That's because none of them is acting", Dada replied.

Miya doesn't give up and what follows is a song of her longing where she sings about the good old times. This provokes Chhaya. She gets enraged to the point where she approaches Miya, knife in her hand. Miya still hasn't given up her efforts.

"I don't see any reason for me to live,
For you've held my life captive", Miya replies

"You have the power to kill, in the knife you hold
But for centuries my story will be told," Miya added with melancholy.

"A weapon you not need to be able to kill,
Just a fair knowledge of Achilles' Heel", Chhaya says with a composed smile.

The play closed with Miya dying and a flash of recognition in her husband's eyes as he cried her name and with it played the background song echoing in Rhea's voice as her husband holds her hand and cries for her death. They finally find happiness together.

When you get to be lonely, you realize...
That life could be hard.
Things don't turn the way you want them to be,
And you feel it is all futile.
But the thing with love
Is that it gets you the one.
When you think it's all done
You get a bright ray of sun...
It's going to happen so quick...
Don't you let go of it.
It's going to steal you away.
Don't you try to resist.
It's a spell, it's a curse,
It can even turn worse.
But the thing with love
Is that it gets you the one.
When u think it's all done
You get a bright ray of sun.

"I may die and touch the heavens, but you still won't win,
In your gloom and loneliness, you'll pay for your sins," Miya said as a final thought.

The audience applause was thundering.

The curtains went down and everyone was jubilant.

"You don't deserve to die," Anusha told Rhea as she made her exit from the stage.

(iii)

She was gone. Joe had sensed it the moment he had seen Anusha waving goodbye to everyone the night before. He knew something was missing the moment he got up in the morning.

He received the letter with his morning paper.

"She doesn't deserve this Joe", the letter read. *"Nor do you, I've endured it all, your stubbornness, your craziness and your fanaticism. You created me in different forms, year after year and I lived the lives of those characters, you said you wanted people to hate me, when you made me seem spiteful and callous, but it never worked because you unknowingly put a fraction of the real me in every character you formed, people loved me again, How could they hate me when the man who made me couldn't? No matter how much you lie to yourself, you know what's true. You never realized that people could love me only because you had made me that way, so in a way they loved you. The applause was for you.*

Let's end this Joe, forget it all, you ought to have peace with yourself, I am quitting so that makes you the winner".

"P.S.: you reached the zenith with this play, I can never beat that. For what it's worth, you're worthy of the best."

Joe folded the letter and suddenly he felt empty. His inspiration was gone, his enthusiasm was dead.

He walked that evening to the theatre and the empty stage called out to him. He circumvented the stage and then took a bow.

(iv)

Rhea searched the whole city; she met everyone who possibly knew Anusha. But she didn't find her. Joe was in hospital after an overdose of pills. Rhea went to see him at the hospital after Dada informed her about Joe's attempt. He failed to recognize Rhea or any other person.

Tears ran Rhea's eyes as she saw Joe's eyes fixed on the door. He didn't reply when Rhea talked to him about the show. Rhea knew she had to find Anusha somehow. The members of the crew finally succeeded in finding her.

Anusha returned to his bedside and Joe smiled, as recognition hit him. Anusha just held his hand and he continued smiling like they had finally reached an understanding. He didn't survive the night.

Rhea walked out of that life, where lives were interwoven with the stage. Her theatrical debut was her last performance. She met friends, love and wisdom in that world.

"I don't see any reason for me to live,
For you've held my life captive."

Miya's words floated through her mind and then came Joe's voice when he said that he lacked the power to kill.

And at last came the conversation she had with Chhaya,

"You have the power to kill, in the knife you hold
But for centuries my story will be told."

"A weapon you not need to be able to kill,
Just a fair knowledge of Achilles' Heel"

Rhea knew she would remember Joe's fixation and Anusha's dedication for years to come.

The Highway

April 2002: The Mumbai-Pune Expressway was made fully operational for public. But I never ventured in that direction before 2006, the year I graduated and was allowed to travel on my own. Before that traveling, which I enjoyed immensely was only permitted within city bounds. On rare occasions, it would include a one day trip to nearby hill stations but only with a group. Going out alone, not an option. What kind of person goes on trips alone anyway?

A person like me of course! I was gifted a car by my brother on the grand ceremony of my graduation. My graduation can be claimed as grand because I had somehow disappointed every single person my parents knew including them as well. I was bound to fail, but I passed. Mom attributed my success to the grace of God and the endless prayers she rendered to Him not to mention the fasts she endured just so that her only daughter should not be the laughing stock of the society in turn turning them into the same. Her dedication was incomparable. People are solemnly devoted to the preservation of social status. Why should she be different?

She wasn't, nor was dad. He maintained his dignified silence on my achievement. It was not an achievement from his perspective. I was and would always be a failure. The fact that

I, the only daughter of a famous heart surgeon (an alumnus of a premier medical college of the country and to add to his credentials, an army colonel) could not even clear the initial stages of the entrance test to his college had stamped me with that sobriquet. I could not get rid of it, no matter how hard I tried. And frankly, I had stopped trying. It's simple, I had the freedom to do what I wanted. No one expected a thing out of me, so a little nickname should not bother me. If calling me that gave him pleasure, I should not deny him; he is my father I owe it to him. Did I mention my brother?

Of course, I did. He is a replica of my father. Ten years older to me, born with a silver spoon in his mouth or rather make it platinum; do they make spoons out of platinum? A doctor in army. In short, he is everything I am not. Sometimes I feel my parents should have stopped at him. It is difficult to imitate perfection. He was perfect. Trying it again on me was kind of over optimistic on their part. But they did. And that's how I landed up here. Is it even fair to have an ugly duckling in a family of swans, a dark horse?

It is not. But in my defense, I am not ugly. In fact, I consider myself quite handsome, pretty even and I am not boasting here. It does not matter anyway. For me it does not. I am not dark either; my mom tells me it's a big achievement in itself in our society. I call it being racist. I mean sometimes I envy the ageless looks of the dark compared to the wrinkles I have around my eyes at an age of 23. But would I be this indifferent, if I was dark? Maybe yes. Maybe no. It clearly depends on the experiences I would have had then. Just hypothetically, guess being ugly would have made my parents totally give up on me. Now they have some hope. Do they?

No. Just to hammer it in, my dad thinks and maintains I am a failure. My mother feels if I find a handsome bloke who is everything I am not which translates into his being born in the exact same astrological signs as my dad, only decades later and he being insane enough to agree to spend the rest of his life with me, I am good. My brother feels that I have overloaded this earth with my presence for 23 long years. That reminds me, he had placed a bet on my clearing graduation. He lost of course big time! And as a memento to the only judgment error in his entire life, he gifted me the car. In other words, he punished himself with the full payment of a luxury car. Did I deserve his gesture?

Yes. No. Maybe. From his perspective, I had defeated him hands down. After I cleared my 12th, not so gracefully I may add, he suggested that I should take up something which is lighter on my brain. In his opinion, my brain was a fragile organ which may stop functioning if I even tried to multiply 24 by 18. (Please don't ask me to, it doesn't fail I agree but surely stalls). And I have a confession to make; I only could memorize tables till 12. Any number above that scares me. So he was right in a way. But I rebelled and took up engineering, that to mechanical engineering, which is a kind of high brow. I am boasting here but from their lenses (my family) it was high brow for me and I cleared it, successfully, that is in four years, with a distinction. Before someone suspects foul play, I must admit that I am not dull. It's relative. As a person, I am smart. Take a family photo and I would look like the dullest person on the face of the earth. Should I have tried to change the opinion my family held of me?

No. A definite no. Reason? As I already mentioned, I owe my father his happiness. I agree that he can be proud and happy for me now considering my success at career but he chose not to. And I choose not to shatter his image of me. My brother is another character. He changed the way he looked at me. Earlier, I can bet he pitied me. God had been so unkind to me (in his opinion). Now, after my graduation that is, I saw something else in his eyes. Gratification? Pride? Surprise? What was it exactly?

Surprise, of course! Picture this: I call my brother the day my results are declared. We both stay in the same city by the way and manage to meet about once every three months or so. He is a doctor in the army and the country not being in a state of war for sometime now, he is stationed in Pune. So I called him and within hours he was outside the gate of my PG accommodation. He demanded to see my mark list. Yeah, right! He thought I was joking. Next day we booked the car. I did not ask for it. It was on his soul not mine. He kept looking at me. And I am not a doctor, but I understand that when a person's pupils expand either he is deeply shocked, surprised or stoned. And I know him enough to say that he had never even touched alcohol, being stoned out of question. So, the car arrived. A red Skoda, whose interiors he expertly got done in beige. Awesome. His only question once we were seated was where do you want to go?

I mattered. So I mentioned the Highway.

"I hear it is scenic." I added for credentials.

"You have never been there?" he asked still in shock. Though I was confused about the source of his surprise, his pupils were still expanded which made me think he still had not recovered from my graduation results a month back.

I nodded in negative.

"Let's go there then."

I assumed that the next question that he asked me was just to kill time. Didn't realize he was serious. Maybe I would have replied differently if I knew he was serious and the conversation that followed would have taken a different course. Nevertheless, it gave me an insight into my brother's character and many others maybe. We should not assume things without concrete evidence. It only results in endless discussions. Does it not?

My experience says it does. So my brother and I were driving down to the highway and he asked me, "Now what?"

So I was like, "What, What?"

"You know, your life, what have you decided to do next?" he asked.

At that particular instant we were passing a movie theatre and as I mentioned I was under the impression that my brother was only killing time, so just to infuriate him I said, "I am thinking of joining the film industry".

Now, being naïve to medical science, I don't understand the elastic limit of human eye. But I swear to God my brother's eyes were thrice their natural size. He did not need to mouth the "What?" I could read it in his eyes along with the expletive "F" word. But he did mouth the "What?" and I replied with my "What?" He kept looking at me.

"You think I am not pretty enough?" I was enjoying this now.

"I didn't say that" he replied a bit shyly. "But I supposed you would do something respectable."

This is what I meant when I said I got insight into his character. He must be kidding.

"You think it is not respectable?" I asked. "People die to meet film actors and just for your information it makes you famous too. No one knows what Aishwarya's or Sushmita's brother does for living. Maybe he is picking stones somewhere (I did the brother comparison thing just to annoy him.) On second thoughts, that could make headlines. But you get my point? The profession has fame, money and respect."

"Not to mention, Lust." He added with a wry smile.

This was war now and everything is fair there, clichéd but true.

"Oh! that's the part of being famous. It's a double edged sword." I threw in.

"Right, that's what I meant. I bet no one lusts the brother's of the film actors you mentioned. That speaks something about the dullness of their profession." He added. Score 1-0.

I was not going to give up.

"So are you jealous of not being lusted at? I am sorry but little chances of someone lusting at your overgrown stomach." (I told you this was war) Score 1-1.

"Jealous? You must be kidding. And just for your information. My stomach is a sign of prosperity." He defended. Score 1-1.

"I doubt the army thinks the same". I replied. Score 2-1.

"I am 33, alright and really sorry if I don't fit into your Barbie world." He snarled and I won. It was like giving up on his part. We were in the last two minutes of the game and he had accepted that any effort now was futile. He was Newcastle without Owen. I was Manchester United with Ronaldo. He had no chance.

That was the end of our discussion. I kept looking out of the window for the rest of our drive. The drive was indeed scenic. For some time, I was lost in it all. Monsoon had arrived and the rains had beautified the natural charm of the place. The shrubs lining the highway and the hills amidst which the highway coiled its way like a giant cobra were obscene green.

It hurt the eye at first, the pureness of the green, picturesque, but once the mind adjusted it was downright beautiful and serene. All this purity protected under the sapphire umbrella of the sky. I could not help but smile. My brother was still mad at me for my earlier comments and he maintained a tight lipped profile with all his concentration on the road. I was in a dream world though totally bowled over by the scenery.

"If it's a dream, don't wake me
In this heaven just let me be."

I sighed.

"What?" My brother exclaimed.

"I am quoting." I said still looking out of the window. I could see from the corner of my eye that he was looking at me with quizzical expression.

"Who?"

"Myself."

"What?"

"Is there a rule which says I cannot quote myself?" I asked instead.

"No, but you're not old enough to start quoting."

"You and your prejudices" I sighed and turned my face away from him to look out of the window. He kept driving and I kept enjoying the landscape.

"Why do people get so ridiculously poetic and sentimental in natural surroundings?" he asked.

"I don't know about people, I am just enjoying myself and the poem just crossed my mind. Why are you being cynical?"

He did not reply. We stopped to refill the car and I spotted my favorite café outlet.

"Let's have coffee". I remarked and he sneered again but followed me to the café. Guess my graduation had made him do things he had never done in his life. But who was complaining?

I was bonding with my brother like never before.

"So complete it". He said as we walked in the café and seated.

"Complete what?"

"The poem."

"I thought you just said it is idiotic."

"Yeah, but you said you enjoy quoting, so complete it".

"I said I was enjoying the scenery not that I enjoy poetry, which by the way I do." I corrected him.

"Complete it", he repeated. I thought he was making fun of me. I remembered our childhood days when as a fourth grader, mom would make me recite the multiplication tables. I would always get stuck at 13 two's are 26 (I remember adding 13 twice quickly). My brother would be reading a thick book and he would be laughing at my predicament. Bet he was doing the same now but I won't let him dampen my high spirits. I had to show off. It was the outcome of 23 years of quiet dumping of the volatile substances; I won't take this humiliation lying down now.

It happened naturally, my voice took a high pitch note as I recited the poem. I was speaking louder than I usually do.

"Such is my bliss that I fail to see,
You're surreal, you're a fantasy
If it's a dream, don't wake me
In this heaven just let me be
Let me be lost, and never be found
To walk away with you, spellbound."

I finished with panache. He kept looking at me and then started laughing.

"What?" I asked.

"Nothing, you are a hopeless romantic". I did not reply. We ordered coffee and he turned his nose up at the overpriced coffee.

"What is with this generation?" he exclaimed.

"You sound like dad," I replied and smiled.

"No, seriously. What's in this place? You can make the same coffee at half the price at home and yet I see this place full. It is like 60 kilometres away from the main city and youngsters swarm in here, just for this overpriced coffee?" He said turning the cup in his hand and looked around. Even I did and that's when I saw the guy on the next table.

He was looking at us. I looked back and we kept staring at each other for a while. After some time, my brother turned to see the object of my attraction.

"Why are you staring at him?" he asked me once he turned back to face me again.

"He started," I replied.

We finished our coffee and the guy kept stealing glances at us, or me?

After some time, we took the exit from Lonavla and drove back home.

I joined a job in my field of study much to my parents' relief. I won't say that I enjoyed what I did. But life was moving on. My brother and I were back to our earlier schedule of meeting quarterly. Now that he had paid for his sins he was happy to maintain a distance from me.

The next weekend, I was free with nothing better to do so I decided to go for a drive. I took out the car and cruised around the city for a while. And that's when I remembered the highway. With the memory of the highway also came the reminiscence of a pair of eyes boring through me. Yes, right it was insane. I keep introspecting a lot but still have no clue about myself. What kind of person drives about 60 kilometres just to catch a glimpse of something which may or may not be there?

One word answer: Insane. A person not in the right frame of mind. I was that person. I reached the café and parked my car. There were no goosebumps, no sweating. I walked in the café and ordered my favorite drink. I did not need to look around. The eyes had followed me right from the moment I had honked shrilly in the parking space till the time I ordered my drink calmly.

He did not stare (very polite). But I knew he was there aware of my presence. This was the time before the ban of public smoking and the whole time I was there he kept smoking amidst sips of his coffee. After sometime, he walked off. And after some more time I walked off. When I reached the parking space, someone had parked very close to my car. Did I mention that I am not a good driver? If I am driving a car I need parking space of a truck. I was standing hapless next to my car with a mental graph of my car, the radius I needed to turn and the road width. The trigonometry was there in my mind, what I needed was skill. That's when the guy approached, the owner of the eyes that had troubled me for the whole week.

He extended his hand and I wordlessly handed him the keys. After he had put to use the calculations I had in my mind, he banged the door and walked off. I should have thanked him?

I did not. I was confused with not even the slightest idea of my actions. He could be a tramp only he did not look like one. He could just have served his time in prison where he did not get coffee. That explained his presence in the café. But he did not look like a thief or kidnapper or killer or rapist. (What all offences do people serve term for?) The only thing that he looked was serene, scary serene.

I was going to come back soon.

Tomorrow.

That's what I did. I drove straight from office to the café. Damn the petrol charges, damn the weather. It had turned stormy suddenly. When I reached the café, it was drizzling. I walked in and he looked up. I was turning into a stalker. I was the stalker. It suddenly made me feel bad and sad about the state I was in.

I did not thank him for his help the day before. It could have been a good excuse to start talking but I did not wish to talk to him. We have had many talks since we met. Don't believe me?

Oh right! I did not mention our chats. I am uncanny in reading eyes. Seriously. I can look through someone's eyes and make out what that person is thinking. Blame it on my upbringing.

When I finished school with pass class certificate, my mom's eyes said, "I am deeply worried about you dear, but at least you are presentable, that's a relief."

My dad's eyes said, actually they screamed, "Disgraceful! What did I do to deserve a brainless child?"

My brother's eyes said, "How do I explain her lack of intelligence to my fiancée? (That's right he was engaged to be married then and that was his only concern, his fiancée looking at him through the failure of his sister.)

All of this happened when we were having dinner. No words were said, but this was the conversation.

So like I said I have had this conversation with the café guy too. When we first met and he stared at me, I said, "What?"

He said, "strange".

I said, "What is?"

He said, "You". That's when my brother interrupted and asked me to stop staring at him.

The next day when I arrived at the café and looked at him, He said, "There you are again".

And I said, "Yes I am".

"You still think I am strange?" I added.

"More than ever", he said and walked away.

When he saw me stuck in the parking he said, "You are strange and funny" and extended his hand to take the keys.

When I reached there the next day in stormy weather, he just said, "I knew you would come."

I was still feeling bad about myself so I walked out before he did promising to never come back again and stuck to it. I did not go there for a month.

I still remember the date; it was my brother's birthday. My parents were coming down after a vacation abroad and we both decided to go to Mumbai and pick them up from the airport. The flight was supposed to land late night in Mumbai and as my brother and I took to the highway I saw the café.

"You want to stop there?" My brother asked and I nodded.

The café guy was gone. I could not see him there. I had met him thrice in the same place and now he was not there. Not a big thing. We took the sofa on which he was usually spotted on and I laughed. Just sitting on his sofa was making me feel funny.

"What?" my brother asked.

I don't know what came into me. Maybe it was the vibes of the sofa but I loved my brother more than anyone at that moment. I felt like he was the closest person to me then and I wanted to share all my joys, sorrows and anguish with him.

"You remember the first time we came here?" I asked him and he nodded.

"You remember the guy I was staring at?" I continued," you won't believe but I came here just to meet that guy again thrice. It was crazy. And now when I am here today accidentally, he isn't here."

He was shocked. "You came here again?" he exclaimed. I was laughing.

"Alone?" he added.

I nodded. "It's over now." I said.

"I am glad it is." He said "Mom and Dad won't be too happy to hear about your latest foolishness." He added grimly. "I did not know you ogle waiters too. I mean, I agree now a days India has many students waiting tables just for some extra cash and he could be one of them but Mom and Dad won't be too happy, believe me, nor am I", he lectured on.

"But he was not a waiter." I defended my stranger friend.

"Then why was he wearing an apron?"

"He was not" I replied trying to recall his attire the first day I met him. That's when it struck me and I laughed some more. I remembered that the first day I was looking at that guy there was a waiter behind the sofa the guy was sitting on and he was looking strangely at me.

"I was looking at the guy on this sofa, not the waiter", I explained laughing. "What do you think I am?"

My brother obviously did not see the joke. His face was deadpan.

"There was no one on the sofa," He said.

"There was", I replied with a wave of my hand. My brother wears spectacles. Thanks to his Medicine degree.

"The sofa was vacant and you were staring at the guy who has just walked in" he motioned to the café door. I looked with anticipation, but he was not the coffee guy but some random waiter with the red apron of the café on.

"I was not staring at him", I exclaimed.

"Oh yeah? Then why is he beaming?" He indeed was beaming. He brought us our order and winked at me as he handed me my cup.

"Was I staring at you some days back when I was here?" I asked. He was taken aback. So was my brother.

"I guess you were, madam" he stammered.

"No", I exclaimed. "I was staring at the guy who was sitting on this sofa that day." I jumped up and down my sofa for emphasis.

"There was no one on this sofa that day", both my brother and the waiter said in unison.

Okay, I needed to calm down a bit.

"He helped me take my car out a day after when I was stuck in the parking. Remember?" I asked the waiter. He looked confused.

"Tall guy, with blue denims, black shirt, jacket." I explained the coffee guy's appearance.

The waiter was looking at my brother now for support.

"What am I supposed to say?" His eyes seemed to ask my brother.

And my brother's eyes said, "The truth".

"Actually, madam that day you behaved a bit strangely. You went to the parking and could not take your car out so then you came out and murmured something about angles and distance and sines and cosines, I am an engineering student so I know," he added with pride.

"Yeah I know. I was trying to figure out the angle of steering to get my car out," I replied. I did not know I was speaking loudly. "That's when he came and helped me, remember?"

"That's what I am saying madam," the waiter continued. "You stepped in the car, took it out skillfully then banged the door, came out again and kept looking at some distance then hopped in and drove off" he was looking at my brother now who in turn was looking at me.

"But I have talked to him." I said.

"When?" my brother demanded.

I did not reply. We reached Mumbai. The flight was still to land so we went into the airport canteen. I ordered my favorite drink and there he was. Blue denims, Black Shirt, Jacket. But I kept quiet.

"What's the matter?" his eyes asked me.

"Nothing", I replied. "My brother is a bit crazy."

"I know", he said.

We came back with my parents.

Next time I met him when we were dining in Pune. He was on the opposite table.

"You should not follow me," I told him.

"I enjoy doing that," he replied.

"Doing what?" I asked.

"Looking at you when you are with your family," he replied.

"Yes, I look stupid. I know. You see it's relative." I explained.

"You look heavenly" he smiled.

I was talking to the most important person and my brother interrupted.

"You are not eating anything?" my brother said, "you look lost."

I did not tell him that I have met the coffee guy and we are deep in conversation.

"Let me be lost, and never be found
To walk away with you, spellbound" I quoted.

Impressions

"Pain is the only pleasure in the world, this is the biggest paradox." Ananya declared with a puff of cigarette smoke touching the roof of our already polluted room.

Ananya—the girl I knew for last seven years. She went to college with me and we ended up staying together in a place termed as the Oxford of the East. An apt sobriquet in my perspective and at the same time a term Ananya hated. She had a definite view about everything in life and always had the last word in any altercation with anyone. The first time I met her was before the turn of the millennium—the first day of professional college. It's strange actually, how sometimes we don't realize when we get close to someone. But with Ananya I knew. I knew it all. Each and every incident that led to us becoming room-mates and inseparable friends from mere acquaintances is etched in my mind.

I was late for my first day of college and this was seven years back, the day I first met Ananya. I was expecting to get thrown out of class for being late but I wasn't. I took the last and only vacant seat in the class cursing myself for being late. As a teenager, I was clumsy and too self conscious. In my opinion I had a large mouth, too small nose and distorted features, all of this added up to my inability to converse normally with people. One moment I would talk to them and then I would start noticing the way people looked at me and I would miss all that was said. For instance, when I walked in that class, the professor exclaimed,

"So this young girl is late on her first day."

I hated any kind of attention bestowed on me. I was glued to the place I was standing on.

"I'm sorry," I managed to murmur.

"Sorry won't do." The professor replied, and then what I heard was, "blah…blah... Name... Blah..." only because I was too busy thinking about the way the professor was looking at me.

"Oh... He is looking at my mouth; I know it's big, now his attention has shifted to my nose, why does it have to be so tiny." I was thinking so I missed out on everything the professor said. Often it was confused with my intelligence. People thought I lacked intelligence, what I really lacked was concentration or confidence maybe.

"Shreya Thakur", I managed to say. By that time, he had moved on to the next sentence and had already asked me to take a seat. Something which I missed only because I was too busy thinking. I did hear people laughing. The professor was kind though, he knew I was just a young, terrified girl. I was shown the only vacant desk at the end of the room and as I walked the whole class turned and looked at me.

And then after about fifteen minutes, a girl walked in skin tight denims, short black top and sequined chappals. Her toes and nails were painted in crimson red. She had an aura of royalty about her. She ignored the stares of the professor and the hooting of the guys who dared. The professor kept looking at her as she shared my desk with me. She had walked in without any permission.

"What? I am sorry, I got lost." She exclaimed looking at the professor. He stared at her for a while. Even the way she said sorry seemed like an order.

"And you did not think it was necessary to ask my permission before entering?" the professor snarled, "Who do you think you are?"

She stood beside me and replied in a firm tone which was not ashamed.

"I think I am a trivial person who is not entitled to interrupt whatever you were teaching."

The professor was speechless and she stood beside me with a calm smile on her face.

"Please spit out your gum", the professor ordered.

The nasty girl looked at him, took the gum out of her mouth with her bare hands, walked to the professor and threw it in the dustbin near his desk. He kept staring at her with a disgusting look on his face. She coolly walked back to sit beside me.

"Next time, ask permission."

"I am sorry", she repeated. This time her apology sounded sarcastic.

I looked at her through the corner of my eye. I was painfully shy and could not in any circumstances initiate a conversation and even she did not talked to me throughout the lecture and the next and the next. She continued doodling on her books without paying any attention to what the professor was saying. When she caught me staring at her she smiled and I smiled back, but still no talk. She was picked on for being disrespectful earlier and the professor asked her many questions during the lecture which she all answered composedly. I was already jealous of her. That was the first step of our relationship, jealousy on my part, indifference on hers.

We went to the canteen together though. There we met some over enthusiastic seniors and batch mates; we were called for the "regular introduction" a term which had replaced the illegal "ragging" but the pattern remained the same. We all new joiners were asked to stand in a queue and a group of seniors stood facing us leering at the scared faces. The routine was simple, juniors were called in individually, asked their names then based on looks, smartness, presence of mind and obedience screened to the canteen or remanded to custody for further humiliation.

The girls before us were asked to do certain casual things like singing or dancing, something which was enjoyable but for teenagers a bit embarrassing. When Ananya and I walked in the canteen, all eyes turned to her and I was relieved. I was selfish enough to let her bear the brunt and go totally unnoticed myself. She seemed unperturbed. Perhaps beauty also confers upon the holder an unexplainable ease and self-belief. At that age she had a confidence which even my 30 year old sister lacked.

"I can touch my nose with my tongue." Ananya said when she was asked to introduce herself. "See", she actually did that!

"What?" the big senior who was acting like a leader of a street gang laughed. "I asked your name miss." He added.

"Well, what's the point, at the end you're going to try and embarrass me so why waste time?" she questioned.

The guy was taken aback but he recovered soon enough. "Are you trying to act smart?" he questioned in an American accent. I still don't know how he managed to don the fake accent, he looked like a villager. But guess impressions are deceptive. All of his friends took an attacking stance before her and she remained calm. I was sweating already. There was a moment of silence. And my mind drifted to the action movies where opponents size each other up and then the drums beat as they pounce upon each other. Nothing of that sort happened there.

"I don't need to try, I am smart," Ananya replied. She pulled me and we walked out of the canteen. So I was with her now. From that day we were seen as a team, No one bothered or helped us in any way from that day. I was also looked at through the lens of her audacity. The seniors had better sense to leave us alone. They perhaps knew that in the circumstances, one complaint could ruin their careers and Ananya sure had the don't-mess-with-me look. On my first day of acquaintance with her, I had moved up the ladder, gratitude on my part, comradeship on hers.

That was my first impression of Ananya—carefree, smart mouth, extremely beautiful and yeah she had guts!

The next day of college she walked in and took a seat besides me almost naturally. We got talking; actually she kept asking me questions and kept on saying, "yeah", "really" at the appropriate places amidst the chewing of her gum. I was subconsciously looking up to her.

When she was looking for a room-mate, I jumped at the chance. I was the youngest in the family and was quite used to being taken care of so it suited me fine. In the seven years that I stayed with her, she never mentioned her family. She would go home about twice or thrice a year but never invited me home. Her room had no pictures of her family and she seldom talked about them. I had managed to know that her father was working in a private firm, her mother was a teacher and that she had an elder brother who was in merchant navy and touched base about once a year. But that was about it. On the other hand, even my distant relatives knew her and she knew each one of them by name.

We had our daily chats after dinner, I did most of the talking and she asked all the questions. When I asked her something she replied, almost precisely but somehow I never got the answer I was looking for. She was fun to be with, but something was amiss. She had tall walls around her which I could not penetrate.

We lived together but had our separate rooms. I never ventured in her room; it was a total no-man's land. I won't say she was a difficult person to stay with, but she was different. She was caring and fun loving. We both shared jokes which only we understood. We were reprimanded by our owner for being too noisy on a regular basis. We had roamed the streets of the town after midnight a couple of times. She knew all of my secrets by then and I knew none of hers. Such was the relationship we shared, close but not two ways. But that was okay. I leaned on her for the emotional support I needed and she was always there, pillar-like to hold me up.

We decided to take in another room-mate so that we could curb our expenses by sharing the rent with one more person and I decided to move to her room with her.

"Shreya, I think there is something which you should know," she said when I was moving my baggage's in her room.

"Don't tell me you walk in your sleep," I tried to joke. She had always locked her room before so I never knew what was happening in there.

"Worse"! she replied.

"Oh, if you talk in your sleep, that's fine too. I am a sound sleeper" I assured her.

"I am a chain smoker." She said and that was the first time I saw guilt in her eyes.

"That's okay," I assured her again. "I knew that."

She did not ask me how; the only thing she asked me was if I was fine with it.

I was not.

"Ananya, I know you have some issues. But seriously I love myself and I don't want to become a passive smoker." I told her.

"Issues..." she repeated and smirked.

"Don't worry I will take care of it" she assured me. I assumed she meant that she would try to cut down or quit. But the "take care" part was for me. From that day onwards whenever she wanted to smoke, she would just say, "Alright, I am walking towards my pyre, anyone wants to come?" and I would walk out of the room. I did not dare to ask her to stop or lecture her. Actually, I tried once and was met with a rude resistance so I stopped trying.

It was the day our final year results were declared and I was ecstatic. We dined out and returned home to chat long into the night. When she declared that she intended on "taking the walk to her pyre" which was kind of a code phrase by then, I asked her, "Why are you doing this?"

"Because as you can see, my limbs are shaking" she replied. She knew when I asked her why, I meant it in a different way but guess she was buying time.

"Not this", I continued, "I mean why you are taking this walk to pyre: as you call it", I air quoted for effect.

"Because I hear, it's the shortcut", She winked at me.

"Ananya, I know you've some problem, can't we talk about it?" I asked.

"No." She replied and lighted her fag.

I knew I had to try. I had been with her for long and loved her. She was smart, beautiful and intelligent. It pained to see her giving it all away like that.

"C'mon Ananya, it's me." I insisted. "Everyone has problems, we can deal with it right? This is not the way." The reply that I got shattered me. But I lived with it and it was a lesson for me to not interfere further. A lesson I refused to learn.

This is what Ananya said, "First of all, you are not my mother, second, it's my life and I may as well make hell out of it. And third, if you have a problem, I believe there are many flats which are looking for tenants."

I did not reply. She apologized for being rude after some hours and I revived my efforts to make her a better, happier person. Coming to think about it, I am not a totally happy person but in my vanity I failed to introspect and concentrated on her.

"Whenever you feel like talking about you, I will listen," I told her. She mouthed a thanks and that was it. The topic was closed, never brought up again. We celebrated our fight and reconciliation with a late night out the next day too. The gate to our apartment was already locked when we returned home and I had conveniently forgotten the keys to the outside gate. With the security nowhere in sight, I was contemplating spending the night on street when I saw Ananya climbing the boundary wall.

"What are you doing?" I exclaimed.

"Getting home," She replied in a hushed tone.

"Don't be stupid, you will get hurt." I complained.

"Shut up"! she whispered and with some scratches climbed the 6 ft tall wall. I waited. Ananya went up our apartment and fetched the keys.

"I had no intention of spending the night on the road", she whispered once we reached home. Our third room-mate had gone to her hometown so it was just the two of us.

"Your hands are all bruised," I said.

She lighted a fag. I nodded helplessly. It was something I could never compromise with. I kept looking for the first aid box and she kept smoking.

"Can you put that out?" I asked as I sat beside her on the floor with antiseptic and cotton in my hand, ready to act as her doctor.

"No", she replied.

Now I was always a meek creature but I was so enraged at that instant that I could have smacked her.

"You need a doctor", I exclaimed instead.

"It's not that bad." She replied turning her hand to examine the gash on her elbow.

"Not for your hand, for your brain," I replied.

She eyed me angrily. I pulled the fag out of her mouth and started dressing her wounds.

"Tell me something..." I started but was silenced by her interruption.

"Don't start it again Shreya." She shouted. "I am tired of fighting you."

"I intended to ask you, that why didn't you climb the gate instead of the wall, it would have been easier." I stated and we both burst out laughing.

It was about 3 A.M.; there was a knock at the door, and it was our neighbour again asking us to be quiet.

"You were a sportsperson as a kid?" I asked next. It was funny that after all these years there were these minor things I still didn't know about her.

She eyed me with amusement before replying, "Shreya, I climbed a wall not Mt. Everest."

"It's the same for me." I was lousy at sports. As a kid, I shunned every physical activity.

"I was good at sports." she revealed. For a second she seemed lost in thoughts. "It was to beat my brother basically. I did everything he did. Played football, karate." she mused.

"And now you are smoking away all the immunity built up." I said. She did not reply and banged the door to her room.

That summer, I met her brother. He came down to meet Ananya and she threw a fit. She was out on her job, when her brother called up and asked if he could come down for dinner and I said yes. Actually when I thought about it later, he made me say yes. How? I have no clue. But I remember when I took the call, I had every intention of telling him to call back later in Ananya's presence, but I landed up inviting him for dinner and worse cooking it too.

"Why did you invite him?" Ananya asked me furiously when she reached home.

I wanted to reply with "because he is your brother" instead I pleaded with, "But I didn't, he invited himself". Now as I looked at Ananya I could easily read the anguish in her eyes, which the voice masked well with anger.

"What time?" Ananya asked.

"8:30 P.M."

"I will be back", she replied, took her purse and slammed the door.

At exactly half past eight he arrived, an exact replica of Ananya, but a few inches taller than her. His face wore a consistent smirk as if he was enjoying himself or at least he expected to in near future. It was looking at the masculine form of Ananya. They could easily pass as twins. I knew that he was about four years older to her, but they looked identical. He had the same light brown eyes like Ananya, was built in a lankier way like her and even had the same dimpled smile. In short, Ananya was breathtakingly beautiful and he was downright handsome. But the similarity ended there, he was very polite, composed and a smooth talker as opposed to the rudeness of his sister. Ananya had somehow vanished so I was left with no other option than to entertain him till my cranky room-mate made an appearance. It was not difficult. He was polite, poised and a good listener. Everything that Ananya was not. I did not even realize that the slowest hand on clock had moved two digits. I was subjected to Ananya's mood swings often and had in a way got used to them by now.

The two hours of dinner that I spent with him flew away in minutes.

"I knew she would pull this off", he said while leaving.

"I am sorry", I said.

"Don't be, I had a great time and I am in town for a week, I will meet her." I was very curious to know the story and though we had met for the first time I could not resist.

"What is it with her?" I asked him.

"Nothing she is just stubborn", he smiled.

"But it looks like she wants to distance herself from you guys, why so?" I questioned again. I felt like a nosy cow, but I had to know.

"It's nothing, just some childhood issues, she still holds to her heart." He shrugged. "Anyway I bought this for Ananya, now you can take it," he smiled and handed me a nicely wrapped packet.

"I'll give it to her," I replied.

"You're sweet," He said and I turned red. "Hope it brushes off my sister."

"That's difficult," I laughed. He was easy to talk to.

"I will come over tomorrow," he said and walked away.

I wanted to tell him to call before coming but I didn't.

Ananya walked in the next day, as if nothing happened.

"If you plan to repeat yesterday, you need to play it for a week", I warned her.

"Thanks for telling me", she replied and started packing.

I was dumbstruck. "You're serious?"

She continued packing for what looked like a fortnight's clothes.

"Ananya, what's wrong in meeting your brother?" I asked.

"I don't want to."

"But why? He is totally adorable". I argued.

That got some attention. Her hand stopped in mid air.

"Adorable?" she repeated. "If you have any sense Shreya, pack your bags and run."

"That's ridiculous." I exclaimed. This was all really clumsy now. "You need to grow up Ananya, grow out of your childhood issues." I played in the dark.

Ananya kept staring at me for a while; maybe she was trying to analyze what all I knew. Some people just cannot mind their own business. I was one of them.

"Childhood issues! He told you that?" She asked me.

I nodded. Something about her appearance was scary; I did not care to find out. She continued packing her bags. "Well, it's up to you. If I were you, I won't believe him."

"What option have I got?" I questioned.

"You are killing yourself with your stupid habit; you regularly come up with unexplainable cuts on your body, which

I know are self inflicted. You refuse to see a shrink and pardon me but act so haywire, irresponsible. Who holds the credibility here Ananya?"

She was taken aback. This must be the longest sentence I ever spoke to her without her interference.

"I want you to be happy, Ananya." I said which was really true. Apart from my selfishness and snooping, I really cared for her. I wanted her to be truly happy. That was the only thing lacking in her. Happiness.

She did not reply so I continued blabbering, "I hate to see you hurting yourself like this. I know I am not smart enough to hold up a conversation with you, you will have it your way, anyway. Maybe you're strong enough and you don't need your family with you. But can't you just try? When someone is extending a hand in your direction, whatever the grudges you have to meet him halfway. Even you know how pained you are. Why do you want to continue living alone and in pain when you can have a life of happiness with your family?"

"Pain is the only pleasure in the world, this is the biggest paradox," She quoted and left the room.

"To damn with your adages", I shouted after her but she had left. I saw nothing of her for a whole week and after, she left town. But I did see a lot of her brother in the mean-time.

He came the next day as promised and I informed him about Ananya's decision.

"And what did she tell you?" He asked.

"Nothing".

He smiled. "Nothing at all?" He asked again.

"Is there something I should know?" I asked.

"Yes, that I have a week off and all my friends are with their families, my parents are on a vacation and my sister is missing. I need company."

"Oh"! I exclaimed.

I accompanied him while he was in town. I saw my actions as a repayment to everything Ananya had done for me. We both knew that there was some problem with Ananya, I chose to not find out what it was and he chose to not enlighten me about it.

I received a letter from Ananya on the last day of the week. I had returned home after a wonderful day with her brother and was supposed to cook dinner for both of us as a farewell. He had promised to return a week later.

I recalled our conversation throughout the day as I climbed up the stairs to my apartment. He had narrated innumerous funny anecdotes from his childhood, a childhood which also included a less grumpy and much happier Ananya. He told me how as kids, Ananya and him had traveled to another city all alone, without informing their parents just for fun. He was delightful, well mannered and honest. That was my impression about him. I could trust him blindly, because he was so sincere about everything. He told me about his life as an officer, the hardships they brought and his eagerness to see a human face after days at the sea. They all made nice stories, embellished with the sincerity of the speaker. I just could not understand Ananya's reason for distancing herself.

The letter deepened my confusion.

"Dear Shreya," it read in the elegant script of Ananya.

"I am sorry for walking out like that. I just cannot meet him. I hope he is back to his wretched ship by now. If not, I hope he is not bothering you anymore, if yes, take my advice and stop. Be safe. I know I am not being fair to you, but you have to understand, I just cannot tell you. Blame it on my cowardliness or blame it on my inability to trust anyone anymore. I just can't. I have to give him the benefit of doubt."

I read the letter and refolded it just as there was a knock on the door. It was him. I showed him the letter and he smiled, his twisted, self-assuring smile.

"I have to know, what does all of this mean?" I insisted.

He just kept smiling. "You really want to know?" he asked and I nodded.

He took my hand and looked right into my eyes, "How about this? I will tell you all about it; let's go out for dinner, Fair enough?"

I was thinking. He was not noticing my too small nose or large mouth as he searched my face for an answer. His face reflected honesty and deep interest ignoring the minor imperfections of my face. Over the days, I had heard every word he uttered without once wondering about the way he looked at me because over the days he had accepted my imperfections. I could trust the way he looked at me and I was sure I even saw fondness in his eyes. That look could be trusted. I could wait. So I nodded. But then Ananya's letter drifted in my thoughts, why would she say "Be safe". I pushed her fears aside as I walked out with him. Ananya was strange, I knew that. She could just be hyper venting. I chose her brother's earnestness over her creepy apprehensions.

"But I was supposed to cook."

"Oh some other time, I guess we have urgent matters to discuss and finalize first," he replied.

"Is it that serious?" I was worried now.

"Yes, you should know what your friend has been through," he replied.

"I am scared." I confessed. I was about to be introduced to my friend, was about to share her experiences. And hopefully get an explanation for her strange behaviour.

"Don't be, it won't hurt you at all and then I hope you are brave," he smiled.

"What?" I exclaimed.

"Why are you so paranoid?" he asked, laughed out loud, took my hand and we walked down the lane.

"Relax" he said with his trustable twisted smile and I could have followed him to the end of the world. I was in a trance.

Ananya:

> I warned her. I told Shreya not to believe him. But there's something with impressions. He is the smooth talker. He can make a man jump in the river. I could not tell Shreya what she so desperately wanted to know without losing my face. I should have told her though. When I saw her again after three months I knew I should have told her.
>
> She was found drugged and full of cuts on her body outside a local pub with no recollection of how she reached there. The way I was found years back in my hometown. The only thing I recalled was the twisted, self assured smile.

Fiction

"It is the most beautiful beach in the whole of Goa, Madam", the agent dressed in off-white capris blotted with yellowish stains, a black beach shirt and straw hat remarked. He was proud of his abode. I looked around. The room looked plain but was clean and it looked like the owner maintained the hygiene of the place. It was a single room, with a balcony overlooking the sea. The furniture in the room was minimal; a single round bed occupied the major central part of the room, the only other furniture in the room included a dressing table, a study table and a chair. Flower vases were placed at every possible location which gave a mild scent to the room.

The agent followed my eyes.

"Good Bed... Madam, original antique wood, Yash Chopra style, round," he grinned. "I myself washing the bed sheets and pillows, very clean... Good soap too...imported. You get it off duty here, floral smell, see", he continued and held the sheets up my nose and I sneered.

"Don't be worried Madam," he continued his efforts. "This place, rented by many tourists, foreigners too...totally safe... Last man here stayed for over two months, from Austria...very rich...gave me this bracelet while going". A gold bracelet shone against his dark wrist. It could have been stolen, not gifted. The agent perhaps read my mind. "I'm joking, Madam," he laughed, "The man forgot it. He was stoned for 4 days before he left. I am wearing it so that he recognize me when he will come back".

Clearly, the agent had no salesman skills.

I continued my inspection. The place looked good, though overpriced. It was away from the commercialized beaches of Goa and was the perfect blend of calmness and activity, something which I so needed then, peace because I wanted to think and action because I would go mad in a slow place. I had grown up in a metro and got easily fed up of slow pace. I needed to feel the movement of life.

"I will take it", I said at last and he looked relieved. A complacent smile played on his lips.

"Thank you, Madam", he grinned.

"What is your name?"

"Thomas Madam, everyone knowing me." He took out a pen, paper and a pocket calculator.

"How long will you be staying?" he asked.

"I don't know... 3 months… 6 months".

"That long?" he questioned and I nodded. He looked disturbed by this revelation.

"Tourist season will start next month", the agent pleaded, "and the rates soar high, I am poor man. My only income is this house. My wife, she runs hotel, you will get good food. Home cooked. But only one month…" he faltered. "You be living for a month, very comfortable, but 6 months, would be difficult…." He did not want to lose in the tourist season, when foreigners swarm Goa and the property rents shoot up. How much can an Indian girl afford anyway?

"Don't worry Thomas; I will pay you at the market price then." I assured him.

"Advance" he looked at me suspiciously.

"Sure" I shrugged.

That pleased him and he started jabbering again, "you have no problem of food… breakfast, lunch, dinner; my wife is a good cook. She will provide it at your room; you will not need to go to the hotel also, if you don't want to. You should try the Konkani curry; never would you have tasted such curry. I assure you."

I only listened to him with half an ear. At last he left and I was left alone to think. It felt great, serene. The voices and the fights were still replaying in my mind but it did not matter. The padding provided by my alert, conscious mind muffled those voices, insults and abuses. The voices came from a long tunnel now and I had learned in the past six months to ignore them.

"You need to take a break." My editor had suggested.

"It's better if I work, I will go mad if I sit idle." I defended. Somewhere I felt that he was writing me off. He had his way at last and he sent me to Goa to recuperate from my loss.

"I am not just your boss but a family friend too and I know how this must be feeling." He had said and I was on the next flight to Goa.

Thomas walked in that night with a tray full of mouth watering food. A rich aroma filled the room as he placed the tray on the only table in the room and stood near the door. The food tasted good and I said so, that greatly pleased Thomas.

"My wife made it especially for you, you want to meet her?" He asked.

Frankly, I had nothing better to do and meeting the wife of this overenthusiastic agent posed no harm so I nodded and Thomas ran out of the room to call his wife. Minutes later he was back with a woman who walked shyly behind him. She was dressed in a floral dress and a smile was playing on her lips. She could be easily recognized as Thomas's sister. They both shared the same easy smile and moist, honest eyes.

"You really make good food", I said and she blushed.

"Her name is Joanna, she is very educated. She teach me how to write," Thomas said with pride and the blush on his wife's cheeks deepened.

"That's great", I said between morsels. I was never good with compliments. There was silence for a while in which both Thomas and Joanna eyed me.

"You on vacation, madam?" Thomas asked and I just nodded. That's the way I conversed most of the time. Lots of nods, many yeah's, plenty of okays and a few alrights.

"Six months", he asked again.

"Yes, Thomas, I am taking a long vacation," I finally said.

Joanna eyed me suspiciously. Maybe single girls looking for an extended vacation was not very common. Her eyes made me uncomfortable. So I added some more information, "I will work from here sometimes."

"What do you work as?" Joanna asked me this time. She looked like an enquiry officer at that instant, but I did not mind her innocent questions.

"I write for a magazine."

That seemed to please her a lot. She immediately left her husband's side at the door and walked in the room to sit near the foot of my bed with knees folded beneath her and looked at me with interest.

"You are a writer?" her voice had taken a romantic tone.

I nodded a yes.

She clapped like a small child. I had no idea what had pleased her to such an extent.

"I thought so." She said, "You are staying for six months right?"

I nodded again.

"Are you working on a book or something?" she asked again. Her eyes showed deep interest which puzzled me. At that moment, if I had said no, it would have broken her heart, so I said yes.

She was fast on her feet and she leaped to her husband who was still standing in the doorway.

"See Thomas," she shrieked, "You say the woman is strange, she is a writer!" In her excitement she forgot that I was still in the same room, but Thomas did not. He looked at her with anger and smiled at me with embarrassment.

"I never said she is strange, Joanna", he said and smiled at me. She ignored him and came back to me in fast hurried steps.

"I tell this Thomas, I want books to read. He laughs at me. You tell me? Books are good! right? I read a lot when I was in school. But then I got married. I cannot afford to read now. But I love to", she went on babbling.

Her enthusiasm was genuine and it overwhelmed me. She was looking at me as if I was some kind of Goddess. I did not have the courage to tell her that I was not a writer. Not in a way she imagined. I just wrote "Bike reviews" for an automobile magazine, that too under a pseudonym because my editor thought that people won't take a girl's review on the latest speed bikes in market seriously. The only published piece of article I had in my name was under the "letters to the editor" column of the *Times* where I had commented on an article published on domestic violence. That was way back in my teens and it seemed ironical now.

Joanna looked around the room. I had finished my dinner. She took my hand and pleaded, "You will read to me?"

"Joanna, you don't trouble our guest," Thomas scolded her. But she continued looking at me and squeezed my hand. What the hell! I nodded back at her.

"It's no trouble Thomas, I will read to her," I said. Joanna's eyes were wet. I did not know what her story was, but the look on her face was ecstatic. "Only if you promise to provide such delicious food everyday," I added and Joanna laughed.

The very next day, Thomas brought me breakfast. He apologized for his wife's demands and said that he would make her understand and that I should not worry myself. I had totally forgotten my promise of last night, but then I remembered the look on Joanna's face and I could have read to her my whole life.

I spent the day in the room. I had no intentions or the energy to go out. Sitting alone in the room was not a good option too; I kept on drifting back to the life I had run away from. The voices I had successfully muted became louder by every passing moment. As if I was walking inside the tunnel, and there was not even a light at the end of it. It was a super massive black hole that could suck me in if I was not careful.

"You think, writing a one page article is a big achievement?" my husband was shouting on the top of his voice.

I kept mum on such occasions. He was not a bad person; he was a good person with a bad temper. We had been married for three years and never had a fight. It was because you need two people to fight and I never reciprocated the insults he hurled at me. I had married him against my own better judgement. My parents had somehow found him through mutual friends and had convinced me that he was the one for me. They had used every tactic available to old, ailing parents of nearing thirty single women to make me tie the knot and I had to please them.

Harish, my husband, was a good man. He understood when I said that I was not inclined to do a 9–5 job. I was just not made for it. When we married, he had supported the both of us from his salary alone. It was he who suggested that I write for the "Automobile" magazine. The editor was a friend of his. I was good at bikes and writing a review would just take some research which I would love doing. That's how I had started writing. Within three months of my articles, the editor suggested I start a "Bike help" column. It worked. I received hundreds of letters from irate customers and young bikers. I was made for this. Back in college, many people asked me why I opted for automobile engineering; a field dominated by males, even Harish had asked me that when we met for the first time. I loved it, that's why. The roar of any engine was like a cry of victory, the speed just thrilling, and nirvana. The engineering that went behind the whole assembly of automobiles bowled me over. Initially, Harish seemed delighted by the letters I received. He had even started calling me by the pseudonym I wrote under. I was basking under the glory which I had never expected to come my way.

Then the insults started. Harish undermined me on every possible occasion. I asked him why was he doing it and he said it was all in my imagination. I chose to ignore his comments but that seemed to infuriate him further. He would say something to irritate me and then keep searching my face for a reaction, but I gave none.

The last straw was when he himself invited his friend and my editor for dinner and started his tirade of insults.

"She thinks she is some famous writer", he laughed.

"But she is" my editor replied, he was totally confused.

"Yeah, right you think writing a one page review makes you Shakespeare".

"You are comparing two totally different things", my editor argued. "And come on, you yourself don't know the difference between spark ignition and compression ignition, of all people you are the least educated to comment on her." That seemed to throw Harish out of balance for a while, but not for long.

"Whatever" he said and walked away.

"What's with him?" my editor asked and I shrugged. I really had no clue.

Joanna brought me out of my thoughts. She knocked lightly on the door.

"Are you busy, Madam? It's turned dark, you did not go out?" she asked me.

I took some time to come out of the aura.

"Are you ill?" she asked again.

"No, come on in" I said.

"You don't go to the beach?" she asked, "It's lovely."

"I did not feel like it, maybe tomorrow" I smiled at her.

She was folding my clothes, without me asking it of her.

"Are you hungry? Dinner is ready", she announced.

I felt tired. I had just been in the room whole day doing nothing. If Harish was around he would have said in his sarcastic tone, "That's what you are best at". But he wasn't, Joanna was and she looked worried. It was a nice feeling, to see someone worried for you.

"Can you bring it in?" I asked her. She looked at me; I was not a pretty sight in my pyjamas and uncombed hair, but her eyes showed care.

"Why don't you come out? We can have food at the shag and then we will go for a walk down the beach."

I felt tired, but just to please this caring, lovely woman, I said yes.

We had dinner and it was as usual delicious.

"Thomas, I am taking Madam for a walk down the beach". She shouted up the stairs of their house once we finished food. He did not reply.

"Must be drunk and asleep!" Joanna exclaimed and took my hand as we walked to the beach.

She remained silent and I was in no mood to talk. After sometime, the silence was not comfortable anymore.

"How long have you been married, Joanna?" I asked just for small talk.

"Ten years, I got married when I was 18." She said and seemed lost in her past.

"What's the matter?" I asked.

"Nothing, Madam." After much coaxing she finally spilled her heart out.

"I wanted to study, but my parents said get married. Thomas is a good man. So I did."

"Oh..." I could not find any other reaction.

"Don't get me wrong, Madam, he is a good person. Just that he does not understand my wish to study. I wanted to be a writer", she went on. Her voice had again taken the passionate tone as she went on baring her dreams in front of me.

"You can still write", I offered.

She laughed. "Yes, I can and I used to. I had a diary full of poems but not anymore." She shook her head as if she was shaking an old painful memory aside.

"Why?" Although I knew it was something painful for her, I wanted to share that pain with her.

"Thomas", she said and looked at me. "One day he came home drunk and I was writing a poem for him, for his birthday, he tore it." Her eyes were full of tears. "That night I burnt my diary and never wrote again." She wiped her tears.

I understood her. I placed my arm around her shoulders and she sobbed a little more. I had been in that strange town for less than 24 hours and I already found a little me in someone. We stood on the beach with my arm around her, two women who understood each other even when no one else did.

"He is a really nice person. Works so hard, everyone in this village respects him for his honesty. He is not a bad man, Madam, but he does not understand me." She defended her husband and then with a wave of her hand dismissed her stupidity, "I can give away my stupid dream to write for him, can't I?"

I nodded. We started walking along the length of the beach.

"I can live with reading good books and enjoying the company of a writer while I can." She laughed and I winced which she did not notice.

"So tell me your story?" she asked and I was taken aback, even scared.

"My story?" I stammered. What was she expecting, that I would bare my heart out to a stranger, that too the wife of an inn-keeper?

"Yes, you said you are writing a book?" she said composedly.

I should have told her the truth. But I didn't. The way she looked up to me was flattering, no one ever looked up to me, or even think that I was worth anything. Three years of my marriage to Harish had raped me of any self worth I ever had. And in my struggle to win it back, I went on,

"You know it is nothing, just a normal fiction book." That did not seem to dissuade Joanna. It did the opposite though. She was excited.

"Fiction, I love fiction, Please tell me the story." She looked genuinely interested. So I weighed my options, I was not feeling asleep and for the past six months had avoided every human involvement. I had only talked in monosyllables and now all the words I had not spoken seemed to brim inside me. It was a safe bet, Joanna was a stranger and she knew nothing about me. So I can as well tell her my story. She won't know. At the most she will rubbish my story off and say "what a lousy book" Who cares? I wasn't even writing the book. So I started yarning and she was hooked to every word I uttered.

"My book is about a girl, grown up in a metro, say Mumbai." I went on. Joanna pulled me down to sit beside her on the beach; she did not even want the distraction of walking and for the next hour patiently listened to all that I said.

"So this girl, she is gifted. At an age of five, she can multiply huge numbers. She knows she is different. When she is eight, she is taken by her father to see the manufacturing of a car, a place where her father works and she is fascinated. She decides that when she grows up she will design cars. But then as she grows up, her dream keeps on taking a back seat as the realities of life pull her down. She gets married.

Her husband is a nice, supporting man but gradually he notices that she is more intelligent than him and that hurts his own self esteem. He takes pleasure out of undermining her in front of everyone. That makes him feel important. She endures everything for as long as she can. She is confident enough to not let his abuses affect her. But then she gets pregnant and she decides that she cannot let the insults go on. Her child won't respect her in an environment where she is continuously being pushed down. So she decides to take her pick. Her husband has to go. She thinks about a way to get rid of him. His one weakness and then she finds one. She is good with automobiles and her husband is not. So she plays with the brakes and the safety of her husband's car and that does the trick. Her husband meets with a fatal accident." I finished.

Joanna was still looking at me, but her mind seemed elsewhere. Maybe she was lost in the story I just yarned. We walked back to my room, Joanna asked me a couple of questions about my story,

"Why did she have to kill him?"

"She was fed up," I replied.

"Oh and then, how about her kids, did she give birth to a boy or girl?" she asked again.

"I have not figured it out yet, Joanna," I replied.

That seemed to satisfy her. When we reached my room she again took my hand, "Thanks a lot for sharing your story."

I went to sleep.

Next morning, Joanna shook me up. The sun was not up yet and I was confused. She seemed distressed.

"What is it, Joanna?" I asked as soon as I found my tongue. She was standing very still near my bed.

"Thomas is dead," she said at last.

"What? How?" I was stunned.

"He was allergic to prawns. I made some last night. He ate them all. He was very drunk, he did not notice." She said. Her face was dead pan.

She should be yelling, crying but she wasn't. Maybe she was deep in shock.

"Why didn't you stop him?" I asked and then it all came back to me.

I was back in Mumbai; Harish had carried his jealousy too far this time. He had insulted me yet again in front of his office mates. The fury was building inside me. I could not take it anymore.

"You can go to hell", I had snapped.

He was taken aback. He walked back to me and slapped me hard. That was the first time, someone had manhandled me. I spent the whole night making up schemes. Harish had to go. I deserved better. I can poison his food. But that was risky. I knew he was useless with cars. I can fail his car brakes. That would pass as an accident. Sleep engulfed me and the weird thoughts stopped. I had won the battle against myself, the next day when Harish drove away in his car. I packed my bags and left.

Joanna was still standing in front of me.

"What have you done, Joanna?" I exclaimed. Thomas's face drifted before my eyes, the easy smile and the honest eyes.

"My wife is very educated Madam, she taught me to write." His voice floated in my memories, as he had beamed with pride.

"I know it was your story, Madam," Joanna said.

I was too shocked to reply. I was never good with disguises and lying.

"I saw your tablets too, yesterday, you are pregnant. It was your story" she said it like a chant now. I could not answer. What could I say to this woman?

I had to get out. So I walked out of the room. I came down to see Thomas lying in the porch below. Joanna had put a sheet on him. His eyes were closed and there was a complacent smile on his face. The gold bracelet still dangled on his arm. I could not bear the sight. I went back up and Joanna was sitting on my bed, weeping.

"That was an imaginary tale, you stupid woman!" I could not keep the anger inside me any longer. "That's what fiction is, you take reality and you improvise!" I had hard time speaking coherently. I was shaking with rage.

"My husband and I are divorced. He is back in Mumbai," I said.

She looked at me accusingly. I did not know whom to blame, her or me?

A Clumsy Conversation

I was back in India. Actually, that statement won't be completely true, because I had never been to India before, so it was more like "I was in India." I mean in a way I was in India before, but in theory not in India on my own because when I was in India, I wasn't strictly in India, my mother was. I was just like two months minus zero, how do you say that I was two months old before been born? Guess that's where my mother would step in and say that she was carrying me for two months, and not in her hands.

Such things scare me but you get the point, right? So let's just say that this was my first trip to India when I was on my own two feet. And not like own two feet figuratively, I mean it literally, like when I use my own feet to walk, not like own two feet where I own a Mercedes or a business empire or something, that is important to know as well, because I own an old Cadillac and I like it and I am clumsy with money and stocks and management strategies. I cannot even manage my own affairs, Business Empire? Not a chance. In short, I can never run a business in this life or any other life if one carries forward such traits.

The only advice my Indian friends back home gave me was this, "Don't act like a tourist. You will get mugged." So I was trying to act as normal as possible. My flight landed in the capital and the realization hit me. I was on another continent, the big green land mass I saw on the globe, the place where most of the population was. I walked back, as normally and as Indianly (I don't know if such an adverb exists, but I can and did make my own ones from time to time.) via the checkout to the domestic airport. I was to take another flight to Mumbai. My Indian friends had some friends and family there and they were supposed to take care of me. I suddenly felt the weight of my bags, because they were loaded with gifts for every single person I was supposed to meet while in India and every distant relative of that every single person, weird.

I already felt like I was put in a furnace. Yeah right, I was given this advice too.

"You will feel really hot." The bloke in my morning classes had remarked.

"I am hot; at least I have been told a couple of times that I am". I had replied. I had a load full of vanity, correction again; I have a load full of vanity.

Now I knew what he meant, but no worries I was fully prepared to deal with the situation. I went in the restroom and used a lot more than necessary antiperspirant. That would do.

I was tired.

The only relief was that the connecting flight was three hours away, I had time to rejuvenate. I took the corner most seat in the waiting section and very soon was snoring, but not for long. I was awakened by someone tugging at my pants! Was it a rodent? Someone was stealing my pants! Scary! My sleep deprived mind explored all the possibilities from spiders to rodents to one of those biomedical weapons people talk about these days. I jumped up and saw a young girl pulling the straps of her handbag from under my feet.

"What?" I exclaimed.

She gave a final tug and the strap was in her hand and I was standing totally dumbfounded. She eyed me furiously and sat beside me. Maybe she was sitting there before too. I had not noticed I was too confused and sleepy to understand what was happening. So I checked my pockets, my wallet was still in there, so were my bags. That was a relief. Perhaps I had moved while sleeping and placed my foot on her hand bag strap. When I stole a glance at her she was murmuring something, I tried to listen, and was dead sure that she was uttering some expletives directed towards me. She looked nice. And not nice in a way you call an ugly girl nice, she was nice nice. And the repetitive nice does not mean that I am being sarcastic, but one look at her and I could just say nice. I was loud; she looked at me again, this time with more antagonism than before. So I looked down. But I could not help myself, I had to look again. She had that kind of magnetism about her. She was reading some book. I tilted my head to try and read the name of the book but I couldn't. Maybe I knew what she was reading, so I tried reading from her page. Wasn't difficult, I had done that a lot in school, the bloke whose answers I copied had a tiny script, but I managed in straight B's. This was a cake walk. Perhaps it was a play; the words on that page were not in paragraphs, they were not centred on the page either like poetry is so it had to be a play. Before I could read a word though, she glanced sideways at me and saw me trying to read. I sat back straight and smiled. Smile works, doesn't it? It did not with her. She closed the book and I still could not read the name, because it was covered with a brown paper.

"Perhaps you would like to read it," she said passing me the book.

I was taken aback. My friends misinformed me. Indian girls are shy they had said. This girl was anything but shy. What does one do in such situations? I rattled my brain for any previous experiences but came out with a blank, which is obvious because no one had spoken to me that way before.

"I am sorry," I said. (Why was I sorry? I wasn't but I said it. I have this weird habit of giving unexpected and futile apologies.) And then there was nothing else I could have said. I pondered over it for a while and "I am sorry" was the best bet.

"No, take it", she insisted and placed the book on my lap.

How was I supposed to react? So I took it, opened it and satisfied my curiosity (It was a play by Oscar Wilde, Classic!) and returned it to her. What kind of a person reads such books at an airport? I mean I had seen people read murder mysteries, romances, business magazines at the tube, but classics? I mean people read during transit to kill time right? It's not like you become a scholar while commuting from one place to another. It's not like you take a train from Liverpool as the dumbest person alive on earth and when the train reaches London you quote Shakespeare. It just does not happen. Guess she was a show-off. But seriously who cares what one is reading? I will only be put off if I see someone reading "how to books..." in full public view. That's like baring yourself out. I mean its equivalent to carrying a sign board saying you are not what you are trying to be by reading the said book. And then the mystery is gone, I mean I won't try to talk to such a person. Such books should just be read in closets or bathrooms, if at all. I mean picture this; if that nice girl was reading "how to be rich and successful in 30 days", what would I say to her?

"Any luck?"

And she would reply with, "I am trying."

Then I would say, "Okay, meet me in 30 days and let's see how you do."

That's a good ice breaker but don't know it falls short of carrying forward the conversation. That's the dead end. What else could I have said? True that's it is just a hypothetical conversation but then it dies there too.

Only she did not look like the self-help books type. Oh yeah, I know the type. She won't read self help books even in her closet, that's for true. You have to trust me on that; she just did not have that look.

What did she look like? As I said before, she looked nice. She was wearing a pair of blue denims, a black—square tee and peep-toe sandals. She had long black hair tied in a ponytail. I would have labeled her as a tomboy but the sandals, the painted nails and long hair made me think otherwise. The square tee could pass her as one of the rock band enthusiasts, I would be the happiest one, if she was, but she lacked that essence too. No dark makeup, no black eye shadow and nails. I could not place her into any of the stereotype, so I was back to my earlier assessment of "Nice".

"Thanks", I said and smiled again. It had to work this time at least, but it did not.

"You're the most obnoxious person I have ever met!" she remarked.

Obnoxious?

Does being curious about a book make me that, I don't think so, I was not even mad at her. Frankly, I had never been angry ever. I just could not. I fail to understand the crabbiness in people. The Americans made a movie for anger management, the bloke who bombed the twin towers must be pretty angry. I had a neighbour back home who spent most of his time yelling on his wife, kids, the postman, the gardener in short everyone who came within audible distance of him. The girl next to me looked pretty mad too. I tried picturing her in the role, you know, piloting an aeroplane, flying to bring some huge famous building down. "Take it", she would say while crashing, the way she handed me the book. Smooth. It was funny. The idea was and I laughed a little. She looked really mad now. See that's the problem with me, I cannot concentrate, my mind goes on wild trips and I have to pull it back to sanity, reality. And the reality was that a pretty nice stranger had just called me obnoxious and I had laughed.

She was eyeing me with interest now. Obviously, I had laughed at been called obnoxious. Who laughs at been jeered at? A shameless person or an insane one. I was none.

"Explain", I said.

"What?"

"Why am I obnoxious, because technically you haven't met me yet?"

"Crazy", she murmured again and went back to her book.

But I needed an answer.

"I was curious", I explained my earlier behaviour.

"Hope you are not anymore", she said without looking at me. She was back to her book.

"About the book, No."

She did not reply and continued reading.

"It's hot here". I tried again fanning myself with my hands. She did not reply. How many ice breakers did I need here?

Okay, this was my status, I was already obnoxious in her eyes with no explanations given, she did not know me from Adam and I would be on a flight in about two hours with no chance of seeing her ever.

I could, you know, I mean what was the potential danger in that. It would just help me keep awake. A little entertainment, so I decided to have some fun and did something crazier, I revealed the suspense of the play she was reading and killed it for her.

"They get to know it at the end", I added pointing at the book. I had been a part of the stage enactment for my school and I was trying to show off. Trying to show I was really well read and smart. I won't call myself well mannered though because I had just given up the end for her. I had just turned obnoxious-ier in her eyes. I was enjoying myself.

"I know, I have read it twice before," she said composedly.

Why would someone read the same book again? That too thrice? I never could. I mean seriously, I was not an avid reader. The only book I had enjoyed reading was...I don't know Superman series maybe but I read it just once. What's the point of reading a book again, when you already know the story, the suspense is done with?

"Oh!" I said. What else could I say?

"Where are you from?" she asked me.

She looked intently at me. The question made me nervous; occasionally I was asked this question back home.

"Where you from?" the bartender had asked me once. He was an ageing fellow with a Scottish accent, the sort who recognize people without a strong, traceable family tree (Mine was traceable, on my Dad's side, but that's okay).

"London, of course", I had replied. The thought that he would think of me as someone not a Brit was distasteful. I was born here, raised here. I had a British surname too. Why would he think I was not?

He had eyed me curiously, given a shake to his head and walked off. It had offended me to some extent. When he brought the drinks, I left him a more than necessary tip to prove that I was a local, which did the opposite I suppose. But the point is, I fitted in and strongly fought against the sporadic strangers who eyed me differently, just because I looked a bit different. Thinking of it, it never was a big issue. Back home, it was not. We had people from all nationalities and we all were Brits.

She was still looking; I could pass as an Indian I thought. I was part Indian too and that was the precaution I was taking from getting mugged, a fact which I vehemently fought against back home and was keen to adopt here. Gosh! I was a rotten hypocrite.

"India," I said and held her stare. She did not say a word for long but kept looking at me.

"What's the capital of India?" she asked.

"Delhi", I said without batting an eyelid.

"What is the space research facility of India called?"

"ISRO".

"What is 259 multiplied by 8?"

"2072" (That took some time but I managed).

"When are the national holidays?"

"26th Jan and 15th Aug—Republic day and Independence day respectively".

"Which movie released this Friday?"

"What?" I exclaimed.

"Ha... you are not an Indian." She laughed.

"What kind of logic is that?" I countered. She just shrugged and went back to reading.

"You mean that I can only be an Indian if I know which movie released?" She did not reply.

"That's insane," I added. I could keep on talking to extract a response from her. She did not respond anyway.

"Really insane," I said yet again and enunciated every word.

"Worked on you." She said at last without taking her attention away from the book. She looked deeply engrossed in it, as if it was a murder mystery and she was at the climax.

"But I am an Indian," I argued. That got some attention; she looked at me for a really long time.

"What you checking me out now?" I laughed.

"You're not", she declared.

What was with this girl? For the first time I had mouthed the words and she did not believe me.

"And why not?" I questioned.

It was silly, I was arguing about my ethnicity with a stranger. But it was not that, the way I saw it, it was not an argument about my ethnicity but about something I said. If I claim that I have just circumvented the globe thrice or that I have just won an Oscar or like climbed the Mount Everest, people should believe me. What's the suspicion about? I trust people almost blindly. If that nice girl was to claim that she is a leading actress I would believe her.

"You tell me," she replied and laughed. A short little laugh, like when you make fun of someone.

"Well," I started, "I am, just a bit out of touch with the movie industry", I air quoted "but I am an Indian."

"Okay", she said and went back to her reading.

"What you believe me now?" I asked and she nodded. What kind of squabble is this? I was all geared up for a fight, with all the arguments up my sleeve and she says ceasefire. Not fair! I kept looking at her.

"I believe you", she said. We did not talk for a while. She was back to reading with a smirk on her face. I could not bear it. I wanted to keep up the conversation.

"Where are you from?" I asked to counteract.

"Central Africa," she replied and smiled.

"Must be pretty hot there", I said sarcastically. She was lying but I did not disagree. I won't. This was the time to prove that one should believe people, the way I did.

"Yeah, that's why I am here; I am the Siberian crane, looking for cooler climate."

"Try USA, its cooler" I replied fanning myself. I had never been there myself.

"Well, I am paranoid."

"Of?"

"Robberies."

I laughed this time.

"Unlike some people, who think that they have landed up in the crime capital of the world, I suppose and hope that the statistics support me here, NY must have more cases of armed robberies than here," she announced.

"Possible".

"Still some people get unreasonable and jump up at being touched and check their pockets after sleeping carelessly in a place with total security".

Okay, this was directed at me. Normal people should be hurt, I guess. But I laughed again. She was making fun of my earlier behaviour and I deserved it. I was paranoid.

"I bet people do that in NY too."

"Right, so you agree that India is just as good and just as bad as US or any other place."

"Maybe, I have never been to USA." I confessed, "I am from London."

She smiled.

"That's what I asked you initially, I am from Mumbai." She replied calmly.

"So why say Central Africa?" I was coming out as a total jerk, with mashed potatoes for brains, but as I said I wanted to keep up the conversation.

"Why say India, you not proud of the place you're from?" She argued. I expected that, the ball was in my court now, So much so for being attracted.

"Are you a lawyer?" I asked instead. I hoped it would catch her offhand. But nothing seemed to perturb her.

"Yes," she replied, "Nice work, I am indeed a lawyer."

"You are going to Mumbai too?" I asked again.

"Yes."

"Business?"

"Yes" she replied. Her face took a grim look, "you see, one of my clients is given the death sentence, I had come to the capital for a mercy plea to the President."

"Oh!" I said. I had not requested that bit of information; she gave it to me anyway.

"What crime?" I asked.

"Murder."

"Oh!" (Again! What was it with me? I wanted to have a conversation and I was coming up with lame sighs.) Was she lying? I mean she looked pretty young for that kind of job. She was not even dressed like a lawyer. I mean I don't think lawyers travel about in square tees with big prints and faded denims. The shoes—well they were classy, different and expensive. But she could not be a lawyer. She talked like one though.

"Double murders, in fact, I just hope I reach there on time, you see she is to be hanged today." She claimed with a serious face.

I almost believed her. Did I? The "she" from her "she is to be hanged today" brought a sense of déjàvu. Where had I seen it happen before? The double murders… the clemency thing… It was a Sharon Stone movie.

She kept looking at me. I knew she was lying, she knew that I knew. But it was about my earlier point of believing her.

"All the best", I said with just a hint of sarcasm. "I hope you succeed in saving her."

"Thank you. Just pray for her."

"I will."

What kind of conversation does one have with young girls lying at every point? I could just play at her game and carry it forward. Or I could cry foul and expose her. I chose to do the earlier.

"I'm impressed." I added "must be such a responsibility."

"Thank you", she said again and this time looked away as she said this.

"So what do you do?" she asked me this time.

Let's see, what do I do? I could be an adventurer trotting the globe, or I could be a religiously inclined bloke who had just discovered the meditation, yoga thing and was in India for the training or I could be a famous cricketer invited for a coach job here, a musician invited for a concert. I was dressed for none of the options. So I decided to explore the movies for a story line. James Bond was shot in India once. Well, it would be too evident. Lies should be subtle. I intended teaching this young girl, how it should be. The perfect art of lying, from the master of lies and that was me. She had chosen a wrong character from a wrong movie. I decided to go with Owen Wilson from *The Darjeeling Limited*. But I could not remember what his occupation was in the movie. The story seemed too good to let it go waste. I was using it anyway.

"Well, I just finished school; I am on a spiritual journey to India," I replied with a poker face.

"Oh, so going to Pune from Mumbai I suppose?" she asked.

Why? I did not know why she asked that? Was the place she mentioned like a spiritual hub of the country? I regretted not finding out about India before making this trip and relying wholly on the friends and relatives of my friends back home. I could not say yes, lest it's a trap.

"No. No..." I faltered, "You see my dad just died and my mother is in India. I have to just go and find her. She does not know. She is at a monastery here." I was back on the screenplay of the movie.

I muttered a silent apology to my very healthy and alive father back home and to my dear mother who had never traveled alone not even to her home country since she married my father 25 years back and took a flight from the very airport I was sitting in then to be with him.

"Oh!" she exclaimed.

"Yeah, I hope she agrees to come back with me." I added with a sad face.

"You're traveling alone?" she asked.

"Yes."

"No siblings." Of course she knew. But she showed no signs.

"None."

I kept looking at her. One of the rules of lying is that you don't leave the vantage point. Stand by what you said and more importantly to be convincing, hold the victim's stare. I am not a regular poker player, but I was a regular liar. She cannot beat me at my game. Her look made one thing clear though, she knew I was lying, I knew that she knew.

"All the best", she said with sarcasm.

"Thank you. Just pray that I find her," I said, took her hand and squeezed it. A troubled young man that I was portraying needed that support.

"I will", she replied and squeezed back.

"That's brave of you," she added after some while.

"Thanks", I said and looked away.

She somehow had the genuine look on her face again, like she believed me.

The flight was announced and we both stood up. We did not realize that we were still holding hands. She shyly pulled her hands back and in that instant I would have believed everything that she had to say.

"See you in the flight then," she said and went away.

If we indeed were the characters out of a movie, she would have been my co-passenger, but that's the difference between fiction and reality, the coincidences in real life are far spaced. I shared my seat with a man dressed in a business suit, who bore a resemblance to my dad (not the one who died, the one who was very much alive and a banker in London). I never saw her again.

My trip was good. I enjoyed the places the friends of my friends took me to. I went to visit my mother's relatives, I know someone must be expecting that I met the airport girl at my mothers place or like I landed in Mumbai, went to my friends place and hey presto! She opened the door. I expected a bit of it myself, but like I said coincidences are far spaced in real life. Trust me, none of it happened. I never saw her again.

The only eventful thing during my trip was the behaviour of my mother's relatives. My mother (again not the one at the monastery but the one back home) had warned me against visiting her relatives. She had eloped with my father when she was already carrying me for two months and all these years she had no contact with them. But against her opposition, I went there. I won't say that I was a welcome guest there; the elders of the family loathed me, but they believed in some old adage that placed me next to Gods, so I was fed, given a place to sleep and respectfully hated. The younger generation was inviting. They asked me a lot of questions about being multiethnic and I ended up inviting them to London, whenever they so desired.

Summing up the trip, I would say it was eventful, hot, chaotic, interesting and after a few weeks I was on a return flight with double the baggage, I arrived with. My bags were full of saris for my mother, Ganesha Idols, wooden handicrafts, glittering jewels and tons of cheap clothes. And a faint memory of the nice girl I met at the airport.

I reached home to narrate the trip to the attentive ears of my mother. She dabbed her eyes with the £25 sari I bought for her when I told her about her family, the way they treated me and all that. She is the sweetest person I know. As a kid I was pretty naughty, but she never complained. She was one of her kind in our surrounding, but she carried herself with a flair I adored. She was nice. Looking at her then, made me remember the nice girl at the airport. Like, she was the younger version of my mother. They were alike. They had the same black long hair. The thought made me tell my mother everything about that girl. She had a good hearts laugh.

"Seems like you really liked her," she said at last.

"Like her?" I was amazed at what my mother saw in my narration. "She was a damn liar," I complained.

"What makes you think so? She could be telling the truth, on the contrary, you seem like a __ liar to me", mom said. Okay she did not say the dash though, but she had a way of saying expletives, a distinct sound. Something like a high pitch cry. She said that's how bad words sounded in her country on television. She never reprimanded me for cursing in her presence after I turned 18, before that I used to be awarded with a slap on the face, then dad made her stop doing that, so my punishment changed to writing "I won't swear again" about hundred times on the board in my study room. None of it helped I would say and when I turned 18, mom started ignoring my occasional outbursts. Anyway, like I said my mind keeps going on wild trips or in retrospection moods. The point is my mother called me a damn liar.

"So you are supporting a stranger?" I questioned her. She should show some kind of solidarity to her family and that was me.

"No, but seems like you like her, because you still remember her after an eventful journey."

That made me take notice, it was true.

"Yeah," I confessed, "She was strange, I mean imagine reading Wilde on an airport then asking me strange questions to prove my nationality. She was strange."

"They all are" my dad remarked as he entered the kitchen and gave me a wink. He was the best natured man I have ever met. And people say I am like him. He was a student when he had met my mother during a tourist visit to India back in the 1980s. Many a times he narrated his story to me, each time embellished with different anecdotes. My mother was also a student then, they had met through common friends and somehow my father could not forget her even after coming back. It was the time before the internet and so dad made another visit the next year. He worked part time and saved a lot to be able to afford the plane ticket to India, which he claimed was very costly. After three years, my mother agreed, by that time dad had already finished his degree and was working in a bank. So against the resistance put up by two families located on two continents, Mom and Dad got married and I arrived the same year to keep them company. That was their story, romantic and passionate. I had gone through the same route as my dad because I wanted to see the country my mother hailed from, my journey was however uneventful.

I went to college that year and soon the episode was forgotten or maybe pushed back into my unconscious mind. At times I remembered her, like there was this time in college when I used to be fast with numbers, faster than the weirdest nerd in class. We were doing this problem in mechanics class and my professor was like, "if you keep on applying the 8N force repeatedly at this point reversing the direction, say about 90 times what would it be?"

"720N force" I blurted out, even before he finished the sentence.

"This proves that you are good at Mathematics, Mr. Jay but the answer I am looking at is a concept called 'fatigue'."

"Oh", I replied and was soon involved in a pleasant reverie with the airport girl. "It also proves that I am Indian", I laughed to myself.

We had this lane outside college, where all the outstation students resided and where you get the best Indian food. I had lived in London all my life, but it was only now that I frequented that place. We befriended an old Indian there and we used to spend about hours there after classes, chatting and ogling girls.

I overheard a conversation there once; there was this group of five girls near our table. They were discussing fashion and my friends and I were overhearing and laughing to ourselves, then the discussion drifted to hobbies.

"I just love reading", one of the girls' remarked. She had an American accent, blonde hair and looked like she was very showy.

"Really?" another one who had short brown hair cupping her face and a superb natural overall tan remarked. She had a Cockney accent and looked like very much from town. Nice.

"Yeah, but mostly fiction and that too modern day, I don't understand classics," the blonde said. My friend mimicked her as we listened.

"I love classics," the brown haired girl replied, "Jane Austen is amazing but my favourite is Oscar Wilde, I just love his wit."

That attracted my attention.

"Really?" the American answered. "You have read all of him?"

"All." The brunette replied with a lot of emphasis.

Against my better judgement I left my table and joined the girls.

"Excusez-moi" I faked a French accent, "I cannot help but overhear you girls, Wilde is my favorite too," I remarked.

The blonde girl smiled and the brown-haired one stiffened. But I managed to confuse them both.

"Puis-je me joindre à vous?" I asked as they raised their brows and I repeated in not so good English, "join you, may I?" and pulled a chair even before I got an answer.

The blonde girl muttered a "Sure" and I replied with "merci" I play my part with flamboyance.

"So where are you girls from? I asked once I was comfortably seated between the two of them. I could be an ass when I want to.

"I am from California" the blonde girl replied and smiled. I smiled back and turned my attention to the brown haired girl, waiting for an answer.

"I am from here." She replied and held my stare. I kept staring at her, smirking at an old memory.

"When was the London eye put up?" I asked and she gave me a faint smile.

"1999."

"When is the Notting Hill carnival held?"

"August weekend" Not precise, but would do.

"What's our national anthem?"

"Long live the Queen..."

"Where does the Prime Minister live?"

"10, Downing Street."

"Which teams are opening the Premiere League this year?"

"What?" she exclaimed.

"Ha... you're not from here." I laughed.

"What kind of logic is that?" she argued.

I shrugged and went back to chatting with the much confused blonde girl.

"You mean that I can only be a Brit if I know who is playing who in Premiere League?"

I did not reply.

"That's insane," she added.

I did not respond.

"Really insane," she said yet again and enunciated every word. "Worked on you."

"But I am from here," she argued.

"You are not," I declared. That seemed to offend her.

"And why not?" she questioned in a perfect accent.

"You tell me."

"Well I am not a football fan. Does not mean I am not from here." Her voice turned croaky.

"D'accord" I said and went back to chatting with the blonde girl.

"What you believe me now?" she asked.

"Yes I think I do."

"Where are you from?" she asked me.

I was enjoying this lot now and my friends at my table were totally confused.

"France, of course" the blonde girl replied on my behalf and smiled sweetly at me. I just shrugged.

She was confused. She kept looking at me.

"Really?" she asked again.

"No, I am from Central Africa," I smiled.

I was good with faces, colored hair and changed accent cannot fool me. She was not that attentive.

"You're a damn liar," I added.

"So are you." She said and we burst out laughing.

"Nice to meet you again", she added in the cockney accent she had mastered.

"Enchanté", I replied and laughed.

Like I said, in real life, coincidences are far spaced. It took me five years to find her again.

The Cinderella Story

It was 11:50 P.M. and I was walking down the lane, alone. I had no idea where the lane led to. The only thing I knew was that I was scared. There was this feeling in my stomach like something was terribly wrong and I could avoid it. I could avert it all if only I knew how to. The lane was lined on both sides by houses with no lights; the balconies were worn out as if no one had ever lived there. Some of them were lined with soot like they were set ablaze. There was something evil about the houses. Not a soul in sight and me walking alone. I could hear my footsteps as I stepped on the dried leaves on the road. Even the leaves gave away under my weight, I had this power to crush any resistance that came my way and then I turned a corner, a lone street lamp had claimed its territory with the semicircle of light at its base at the end of the lane. And I could see a house, white as pearl where the light of the lamp merged into darkness, a total contrast to the dark, murky houses earlier and so I start running to reach that place, to reach it before the strength in me fails me, before my legs give away. I run as fast as I could. But the house is like the horizon, I keep running to reach it, touch it and it keeps shrinking back. No, it was not shrinking back it was there, where I saw it, at the end of the lane but I could not reach it. I tried harder, increased my pace,

I was heaving now, panting for breath, trying to reach my home but it was unreachable. And then there was a big noise, a tick and the clock struck twelve. I fell down on my knees, I was defeated.

I woke up with a start; I have had this dream for like forever now, every time I woke up when I fall down on my knees in the dream. The nightmare had been my constant companion, I was used to it, and in fact if I did not have that dream more frequently I would start imagining things. I had to run, see the murky neighbourhood I walked in at nights, I would miss it if it failed to enter my thoughts for even two days at a stretch. Such was my involvement with that dream. In my free hours I would surf the internet to try and find such places, as if that place held a key to unlock a great mystery in my life. There was something in that white house that was rightfully mine and I had to get it. My friends were tired of my antics, its simple actually, the first time you narrate a supernatural, freaky thing it makes the audience's hair stand at their end, goose bumps appear. My dream had that kind of aura. It was scary, but then I killed it. My friends started being less of impressed and more of irritated when I turned up again and again with the same story, I could not help it, I had been having that dream almost daily, I had to do something about it. I had to find new friends whom I could narrate the incidents of my dream to, someone who would understand my quest, my need to find a meaning to that dream, someone to join me in my search for that place.

My life as a gynaecologist did not offer me that privilege, my last holiday was three years back, when I had attended my best friend's wedding in our ancestral village in the south of the country. After that I never felt the need to take time out for myself. My best friend at 27 was considered too old to get married but she had managed before her birthday and saved her family from the disgrace. That was three years back. We both were of the same age and now my chances were nil. So it was plain logic, marriage was a bliss which would never happen to me so I stopped going to other people's weddings too. The fact that gradually people had stopped inviting me is another story which I never pondered upon.

I had this colleague who mastered in extracting personal information about other people, no, he was not a psychiatrist but in matters of the heart and brain he could bring the highest paid psychiatrist to shame. He had an opinion about anything and anyone and the saddest part was that he was always right. I narrated my dream to him and he took his stance, the thinker. I liked him immensely because he was the only person who asked me about it on his own. He never gave up. As a result we had been through lots of speculations:

"Did you ever lose your way as a kid?"

"No."

"Any childhood trauma, you know what I mean?"

"No."

"Did you fell down from stairs ever?"

"No."

"Did it so happen as a kid that you felt really alone with no one to turn to, no friends?"

"I had plenty of friends."

And so it went. Every day he came up with new theories. The fact that none fitted the bill troubled him more than it bothered me. Many a times it so happened that I was in the operation theatre, he was an anaesthetist and would be present for every operation and he would come up with something as bizarre as, "Did your parents love you?" It was difficult to stop him. I wanted to scream with, "of course they did. That's what parents are for, loving their children are they not?" and I would just look at him and try to roll my eyes.

"Right, not the time", he would mutter but repeat the same procedure over again the next time.

Everyone has some fixations, mine was the dream I mentioned. The anaesthetist friend was fixated with helping me and for that matter every living being around him. He would give food to stray animals, water the cactus near our hospital reception and try to find solutions to every problem. The fact that he was divorced with no custody over his kids was never mentioned, it was a reality not a problem so he could not solve it. We once had a patient, a beautiful 35-year-old woman with two daughters; her husband was fixated with having a male child. Not that we could help, but it was a topic of discussion for long. He was a senior government official with international education and all he wanted was a male child. The wife was the perfect example of modern day woman but only in looks, she supported her husband fully and was ready to try anything from *in vitro* to ancient calendar planner that would aid them. And my anaesthetist friend came to their rescue. Not really, but he came to our rescue. He held a three hour long discussion with the family and convinced them otherwise.

"We should shift you to the psychiatric ward", a senior doctor remarked at his achievement.

"Well, if they did not have two daughters already I could have convinced them to try for a female child," he replied.

The irony of the situation was that whatever he said was short lived. He could convince people but his words were like the painkillers whose effect wears off after some hours and then one has to repeat the dose. Sadly, the couple did not repeat his dose and the wife was admitted a year later. To cut a long story short, she died. This greatly affected my friend. For weeks he lost all interest in understanding my dreams or giving free advices to everyone within an ears shot. He even stopped watering the cactus and that was the biggest loss, the shrub turned brown to show its disapproval. It was not difficult to bring him back though.

"I am concerned about my son, he is never home. Don't know what he does with his time." An irate parent and a very senior doctor remarked at lunch and our man was at her rescue.

"How old is he?"

"Seventeen."

"Any signs of alcohol use?"

"No. I don't think so."

"Does he respect you?"

"Yes, just that he spends so much time out that we feel he does not live with us anymore."

"Oh don't worry", he said with a wave of his hand. "When I was growing up I used to be living at my friends place. We had wild late night parties, drinking beer and gossiping. That went on for three or so years in my teens but everything is fine now. It was just a healthy guy time with my buddies. I turned out to be okay." He finished and I bet the lady was more concerned than pacified. The only positive outcome was that we got our free advisor back.

"So I have a new theory," he said one day. Luckily we were just two of us in the hospital canteen and so I could listen.

"Were you like trying too hard to be what you are today?" he went on without waiting for my approval.

"I did not try too hard, but yes I wanted to be a doctor." That seemed to please him.

"And do you think you have not achieved what you set out to achieve?"

I eyed him curiously. He returned my stare. This was the situation: I was his senior in profession, earned more than him and was five years younger to him. I did not want to say it all loud and hoped that my stare would work. The message got through eventually.

"You are not married," he said.

"Does not matter to me."

"Consciously it does not, but subconsciously it does."

"What?"

"Maybe the running part is for you chasing your dream and not quite reaching it."

"I have reached it."

"You have reached your dream, which you saw professionally, but ideally you have not achieved perfection."

"I never aimed for perfection."

"Oh… that everyone does."

"I enjoyed everything I did and so the final destination is not perfection."

"Then what is it?"

"There's no final destination, it's just a life worth living and enjoying at every moment."

"While traveling towards perfection..." He explained in his usual nonchalant way, "Everything is aiming towards perfection; the universe is expanding to reach the perfect size."

"Nonsense" I claimed.

"No dear, Physics."

"The same thing," I winked at him. He was in no mood to give up though.

"Think about it, it fits, your dream is you running towards perfection." It did not take me long to think about it. It was rubbish.

"That's the most plausible cause of your dreams."

"Dream", I corrected him. There was this just one dream.

"What do I do to get rid of it?" I asked again.

"Achieve perfection in your life."

"How?" I was the blind follower and he was my messiah now. It was strange because my messiah was not perfect himself. His personal life was total mess and his appearance at work labeled him the most unreliable doctor.

"Achieve all that you wanted in your life."

"I wanted to be an astronaut. That's not possible now." I laughed.

"You got to be reasonable. Maybe the dream would stop once you get married," he mused.

"Really? That's perfection for you? Yours wasn't perfect." I could not refrain myself from passing that comment.

"I am not the one having nightmares." He responded.

"True," he was just trying to help me.

"What about the guy you liked back in college?" He knew quite a bit about me because we had attended the same college, he was my senior and had also served as faculty after finishing his degree. So I had known him in capacity of a senior, teacher and now a friend. The guy he mentioned, Dr. Mayank was my crush back in college, I was in my first year and he helped me a lot. Then he left to do his MD from Russia and we lost touch. It was nothing serious, just a bit of attraction from a teenager towards a senior, good looking person.

"It was nothing serious."

"You never gave it a chance to become serious."

"Everyone in college knew that you loved him," he added.

"No. I was just attracted to him and it's just a matter of perspective, a common error, we often misunderstand a deep rooted attraction for love, only because we spend so much time thinking about it."

"And now?"

"Over the years I never remembered him until the moment you mentioned his name." Which was a lie because I remembered the smart presence of Dr. Mayank every now and then. I had off-handedly claimed that it was an attraction, but the kind which I was not over yet.

He seemed lost in thought but only for a while.

"What about Dr. Pai from third floor?" he asked next. Dr. Pai was this shy south Indian doctor in the dental department. He smiled a lot and had perfect set of teeth that shined against his dark complexion, a perfect contrast and I had said so recently.

"What about him?"

"He seems to like you." That was true; he came down often to our department for a chat and enjoyed talking in my mother tongue with me. He seemed honest. But I never felt anything other than a pain when he came down because he refused to leave early. At such times, I was selfish enough to pray for many patients without any concern for the population growth.

"But I don't."

"Give it a try."

"My life is perfect without that trial."

"Why are you so hesitant?"

"Oh... I just hate him. He is so irritating. The way he goes on and on trying to impress with the language. For God's sake, can't he speak English?"

"Relax; the guy likes you that is all."

"Oh... but he should realize that I am not interested. One sided love is like leprosy, last stage. It disfigures you. The sooner it is treated the better."

My friend took the stance again, the thinker.

"You should try regression therapy, the answers lie in your past, some suppressed memories that you see in your dreams." He took a pause and I jumped in my chance to interrupt any further speculations from his mind. "I have to get back home." I said, took my bag and ran.

That night was strange, because it was 11:50 again. I was running and the houses looked even spookier. I kept running and someone called me, this was a welcome change, not for long. It was Dr. Mayank. He was leaning against one of the balconies, covered in soot.

"They burnt me Shraddha", he shouted, "keep running." So I kept running and then there was Dr. Pai on the end of the road, I had taken the turn and he was standing near the streetlamp grinning, but his teeth were absent. The perfect set, gone, his nose and hands were disfigured too.

"Shraddha, see, you are not scared *na*? Please don't be scared." Dr. Pai said in his heavily accented voice. I gave out a shriek and then I saw my white, pure house. It seemed to call me. So I ran as fast as I could. My anaesthetist friend was standing at the door; I could make out his silhouette. It was him.

"Run, you can make it." And then the tick of the clock as I fell down on my knees, defeated. I woke up all covered in sweat. It had never happened before.

Next day I reached the hospital, my anaesthetist friend had not come yet and I was waiting eagerly for his arrival, to tell him about the modified dream. The head nurse came in after sometime.

"There is this woman admitted last night, her blood pressure is going low, I guess you need to operate on her." She announced.

"Is she stable?" I asked.

"Yes."

"Okay, take her in the operation theatre and call Dr. Pandit, see where he is, we will need him." I announced. Dr. Pandit was my anaesthetist friend.

The nurse eyed me like I had gone mad. Then her look changed from anger to surprise to worry.

"Doctor, you don't know anything?"

"What?" I asked.

"Yesterday night, Dr. Pandit and Dr. Pai had gone out and they met with an accident. Dr. Pai's hands got crushed under the truck that passed over them and he lost all of his front teeth too. Strangely, Dr. Pandit is all well; he did not have even a single scratch on his body."

That was a shock to me.

"Where are they now?"

"Dr. Pai is in the special ward and Dr. Pandit is with the police. He has taken the day off." The nurse informed.

I immediately rushed to the special ward, Dr. Pai was asleep. His face was all swollen up.

"All the teeth gone." The nurse informed me. I nodded.

"They cut his fingers too. He is diabetic." She said again and I kept looking at the man lying so helpless on the bed. The lanky face all swollen up and disfigured. He woke up and smiled, a toothless smile I so vividly remembered. How can it happen? I turned.

"Oh! you are scared, just go." Dr. Pai said. The words came out all wrong from his wounded mouth but I knew what he wanted to say. I had heard it all before. I turned back and smiled at him and spent the next hour chatting with him in our mother tongue.

I tried calling Dr. Pandit but could not reach him. His phone was switched off. All of this had made me really uncomfortable. I needed a dose of tranquilizer. Then something struck me.

"What time were they brought in yesterday night?" I enquired.

"About 12:30," the head nurse informed me.

"That means they met with an accident at midnight?" The conversation with Dr. Pai had informed me about the location of the accident so I could calculate.

"May be." The nurse replied and I redialed Dr. Pandit's number, still no answer. The next thing I did was to search for Dr. Mayank's number. It was impulsive; I somehow managed to trace him back in the capital city. When I called, no one answered the phone. I was frantic so I started calling all my classmates, the people I had lost touch with since last few years. No one seemed to know. Everyone gave me a different version, if they knew. Finally, one of my classmates gave me his wife's number. That was a shock; she said she had worked with his wife while Dr. Mayank was in Russia. So he had married right after the college.

I dialled that number and a woman answered. When I introduced myself, she laughed. "Of course I know you Shraddha, Mayank spoke about you often before we got married."

"He did?" I was pleasantly surprised. "What did he say?" I was curious now.

"Well, that you are very intelligent and far beyond his league." I could hear the smile in her voice.

"What?" I exclaimed.

"Oh don't shy now, everyone in your college knew that he had a crush on you." She said, she also said that Mayank had been honest enough to admit it to her before marriage. I was shocked because all these years I thought it was the other way around.

"Well he never said that to me." I managed to say. If only he had, I would have been at the other end of the phone.

"Well he believed that you would never say yes, you had big career plans for yourself. And then love is only good if it's reasonable, unreasonable love is dangerous. It makes one insane," she said.

"Well, it is a surprise to me" I confessed, "Anyway, can I talk to him right now?" I asked.

She was lost for words.

"Don't you know?"

"What?"

"He never came back from Russia."

"What?"

"Well, there was this huge fire there and they lost him."

I kept the receiver down. It can't be happening to me. I had my head in my hands when the phone vibrated with a loud shrill. It was Dr. Pandit calling.

"Shraddha, what would you say if I said that I am alive now?"

"Sharman... just hear me out..." I tried to interrupt but there was no stopping him.

"No, you listen to me Shraddha, I have been a fool. I know... It all made sense yesterday night, when we crashed and I was saved, I realized what a fool I am. I wasted my life living the lives of other people hoping that it would somehow put sense into me. I watered the damn cactus, what a waste! I have lost my wife and kids, only because I did not care enough. I went there... yes... that's where I am since morning. They won't have me back. But I am not regretting it. I will start afresh. I am leaving to start afresh. I am going."

"Sharman... it's about my dream, please listen me out." I tried again.

"No, Shraddha, you listen... your dream is just a dream. Value the people around you. Dr. Pai is a nice man, don't hate him. I would always remember you Shraddha. Bye."

He did not give me a chance to speak. I was dumbfounded. I tried his phone again, but he had switched it off. I sat there for endless hours, the shift changed and the head nurse came in, "Dr. Pai wants to meet you." She informed.

I went in to the ward and Dr. Pai was sitting upright on his bed. He smiled the toothless grin as I walked in.

"Shraddha, thank you." He said. I was lost. "All these days, I pestered you a lot." I tried to interrupt but he held his bandage clad hand, "I know, you were thinking what this funny man is doing, coming to my office and talking in native language." He smiled again. I had enough experiences for a day, but guess I was bound to know this. He went on, "I always thought you are smart, intelligent woman and you hated me, I enjoyed that... But today you showed that you care. I would never forget this. My career is over now..." he said raising his bandage clad hands "... I would go to village soon, but just want to tell you that I never met a remarkable woman like you. Let God give you all that you desire."

Dr. Pai finished his speech and I had tears in my eyes.

"What is the time?" I asked him instead.

He was confused. "11:50 P.M., your shift is over at 8, why did you wait so long, it's...."

I did not listen to what he said; I was already running, running through the stairs and the roads.

"*Bhaiya, CST chaloge?*" I asked the sleepy taxi driver. He looked at me for about a minute, analyzing me for I don't know what, but I snapped, after a few expletives, I was running again. It was late at night and most of the houses were dark. I kept running, my legs were giving me away and all of my life playing before my eyes, like I was floating, it was my end. My brain was working overtime though. I was running away from my past which I had held so dearly, the dark past which had nothing left in it but dust and soot.

I ran past the flora fountain and the showering water, the lights reminded me somehow of the man on the hospital bed whose smile had lightened my day for months now, but I failed to appreciate it. I kept running and stumbled into CST but I did not know where to look, I was running like a mad woman on the platform, I tripped over a beggar sleeping on the side and landed on my knees. The LED display before me showed 00.00. I was late, defeated again.

Then under the display, I saw Dr. Pandit standing. He was smiling. I pointed at the LED and his smile turned into a grin.

"The answers were not in my past, it was my future I was foreseeing," I said getting up on my feet.

He looked confused.

"I had many lessons to learn before I reach here, that's why I could never reach my perfect home in my dream."

"I am lost," he said.

I smiled. It all made sense to me now.

"The final destination is perfection but we need to learn a lot before we reach there. I agree with you now."

"What did you learn?"

"Letting go of my past, because it's all soot, nothing is left of it, if I wandered there for long I would be running in circles in the dark, no hope, no life. And if I chose to live in those places rebuilt from ashes, I can never get rid of the darkness which would prevail underneath."

"Hmmm..." he said.

"The present is my ray of hope. I could have stayed there, complaining about the gloominess of the light, and regretting not having turned a corner to explore a new horizon at the same time I needed to respect that light because it was my savior from the dark. I learnt it finally and that's why I reached here today and found you."

"So what are you going to dream about tonight?" Dr. Pandit asked me.

I had no answer. I had learned to let go.

Confessions

Falling hurts, be it in love or from a great height or from a lucid dream into reality. And it hurts more when the reality is a perfect world which you cannot trust. Perfection is scary in a strange way, while imperfection is comforting and reliable. Everything had to have a chip for me to believe in it. So I rejected the goodness in Arjun because I did not trust him, he was not tainted enough and hence he was not real enough.

Ten years of our togetherness and I doubted his presence, doubted every word he uttered. I laughed at his innocence and he laughed at my cynicism. I was wild, even as a fifteen year old I was more outgoing of us two, more adventurous. He was just a shy, awkward boy who never initiated a conversation. We met when we were lousy fifteen year olds too conscious of our existence at a guitar class. Over the years, he mastered the instrument and I was struck at the basic chords but we managed to stick together. At our first meeting I laughed at his shy demeanor as his parents talked to the teacher about his progress with the instrument, he won't speak and he won't look up from his notes. All of it made him strangely attractive in my eyes. It took us three weeks and four chords to start talking in the first place which can be put as me talking to him and him replying in monosyllables. That graduated to occasional coffees and he opening up to talk about himself but still shy enough except for the part where he talked about his football matches, the only thing he was overtly passionate about. And I listened, not because I was interested in the game, but because I liked listening to him. It made me smarter, I was the only girl in town who understood football in detail, knew when which match was to be played, and knew all the rules, all the players, all thanks to Arjun. It amazed many people and it pleased me.

I also understood when he said his family was moving to another country where football was a passion, where he would get a chance to explore his dream and maybe play professionally.

Six months later, I stood at the airport waving goodbye to a teary eyed lanky boy as he turned back again and again to say good bye. Bye, Bye.

(ii)

Long distance relationships never work. They were invented by World War soldiers who went away to defend their countries from overly ambitious politicians and came back to cheating wives sometimes while they themselves had their amount of fun at houses in Italy and France. Not that anyone minded and not that anyone even mentioned it again, but it was not for me. I was liberal in thoughts not in deeds. So I cut off all ties with Arjun. Initially he wrote long letters about his new world, a world which was alien and exotic to me. With the advent of the internet it advanced to long emails and bulky attachments of his every new outing there. I fought against his every effort to reinstate our bond and read his long letters and later emails with as much interest as I paid to my syllabus books and that was not much. For me he was just an old friend who should send an occasional birthday wish and expect the same. The fact that he invested a lot of time in me and expected the same was upsetting. People moved on in life, no one holds back to old ties and old friends, but he did.

We had grown up together in a way. Our conversations had graduated from the childish talks of bollywood movies, football and music to a more personal level. Now we talked about relationships, the idea of falling into one and all such things which aren't comfortable in a face to face tête-à-tête but quite entertaining when the presence is virtual. Arjun had a strong virtual presence in my life. My childhood friends knew about him and often enquired about his whereabouts. His description had changed from being my shy friend to an exotic persona. And I was attracted to him, used to him. It had nothing to do with the fact that he was my first childhood crush. I vehemently denied the claim whenever my friends teased me about it

"Remember how you never missed a single class when he was here?" My friends teased. It was true, more than the learning experience I never missed the guitar class because it was the only time I could meet him. After he left, I left the class. That was the problem with keeping in touch with your childhood friends; they make sure one never forgets the embarrassing truths of growing up. My embarrassing truth was that I had a huge crush on Arjun. But that was then, when we stayed in the same colony, walked back together from our respective schools, saw our first movie alone together. I called him whenever I was upset for something as trivial as breaking a fingernail and he made sure to be there in the shortest possible time. But time changes, and with it people change too. He wasn't that important to me now, with the passage of time even his face was getting blurry and so were the memories of our time together. I often taunted him about his escapades in a new happening country and he laughed it off sometimes denied them but I did not believe him. In my eyes, he must be having a great time there and I was happy for him. I had changed, sadly he had not.

Years later when I stepped in my youth he said he wanted to meet me, so he came back home. I did not resist and he traveled a thousand miles as I waited uninterested on the international airport. My sentiment was soon reversed when I saw a very athletic, handsome and still attractive Arjun walk towards me with a familiar smile playing on his lips.

More than me, my family was happy to see him; he was polite, well behaved and still shy. In my cynical world he was a fake. So I questioned his every motive, his every move.

"Let's go out for a drink." I suggested, the night he arrived.

"I don't drink." He replied and I laughed.

"Seriously, Arjun, you need not do this." I smiled.

"Do what?" question in his eyes was genuine and my sarcastic eyes ignored it.

"Try to impress me." I replied and laughed again.

"I am not."

"Yeah yeah, I don't drink, I don't smoke. I have stayed in the most happening city in Europe for eight years of my life without a girlfriend, with absolutely no wrong doing, with looks like that; I lived like a saint, who would believe you, Arjun?"

"I thought you did." He replied with a stunned expression.

"You never give up, do you?" I mocked him and started walking down the lane.

"Give up what?" he questioned me as he fastened his pace to keep up with me.

"The façade."

He laughed and we walked in silence.

"I am coming back." He announced after we had walked a few more miles.

"Why?"

He just shrugged.

I turned to face him completely. He could not be serious.

"I have the same prospects there as I have here and I miss here." He offered as a means of explanation.

"No one misses here, Arjun, you're not coming back. End of discussion." I made the decision for both of us.

The next day he booked his tickets and the next week he flew back.

In that week, we met almost everyday, it was hard not to meet; he was staying at my place. And it was hard on me to see him move comfortably in my house, treating my parents like his own, giving football tips to my younger brother and be a part of the house, my house.

Everyone fell in love with him, trusted him except me. I needed some extra assurance; maybe I needed to trust myself first before I could trust him.

I drove him to the airport.

"You know why I had come, Resha." He said as a matter of fact as I parked in the airport parking.

I nodded.

"Why is it that you find it so hard to believe me?"

"I don't know."

"If it is so hard for you to believe me, there's just one way, you come to my life, and see that it is for real. No façade that I put up for your sake. It is me."

"Come to your life, as in?"

"I don't know, if you are that scared, take your time, there are many courses. Take an admission and come over. You can see me for real."

"And then? Where does it go from there?"

"You know where."

I knew where, but I did not want him to say where. I was plain Jane, he was Prince Charming, we did not belong together and I did not want to accept this fact to him. My only defense against this fact was my sarcasm and my attack was on his saintliness, I used both to the maximum.

"Here's the deal..." I suggested instead, something I knew would hurt his sensibilities. "I would come, but with a time frame and then I would come back, you won't talk about the time I was there to anyone and I won't either and we would never see each other again."

He was shocked. It was evident from his face. He kept looking at me as if he was not looking at me, his friend of eight years but a whole new person, maybe I was a whole new person.

Did I mean the offer?

Yes I did.

"And what do you plan to get out of it Resha?" he asked me still totally flabbergasted.

"Its not for my sake, Arjun, it's for yours. You think you see something which is not there; it's for you to see the reality, for you to get over your fixation." I remained calm.

"Does forever mean nothing to you?"

I did not reply.

Forever meant everything to me when it was used in a sentence framed "this is not going to last forever" forever only had a meaning with negation. Without negation it had no meaning. It was like zero, without any meaning when it stood before a number and added all the depth after a number in my case after the word "not".

What Arjun and I had was "not forever."

In the parking of that airport, Arjun took my hand and for the next few minutes I compared the pinkish skin tone of his hand against the tanned brown of mine, the softness of his to the roughness of mine, and my mind played the words "not forever".

The email arrived a fortnight later.

"*I thought about it*" it read, "*I cannot do it to you. You deserve the dignity of my lifelong commitment. I don't understand your cynicism, there never was a façade. I hope I can convince you of that. I can convince you of one thing though that I would be there whenever you decide otherwise.*"

I read it with as much interest as the previous hundred mails and returned back to my life.

(iii)

December of the next year and next few years, Arjun kept his words, he kept coming back and faced my opposition. He did not give up, nor did I.

Every year was the same, with almost the same conversation. I won't allow him to give up his flourishing career and come back home. I turned 25 and still had not met anyone, not because I had Arjun but because I was too full of sarcasm, I always managed to push people away with my tones of sarcasm. I wasn't complaining either. I was also a bit of schizoid, too happy in my own Barbie world, anyone who wanted to be a part of my world had to climb up many steps, clear many hurdles and people gave up, everyone except Arjun had given up. I wanted him to give up on me, move ahead in his life. I had not promised anything to him, but he refused to grow up beyond our time together as fifteen year olds. He refused to believe that we had grown up to be two different people. I was the cynic and he still was the romantic. I knew I had to create a make believe world, assure Arjun that I had moved on, maybe then he would too.

I first met Mudit at a childhood friend's marriage. He was an average guy with a fake accent perfected at BPO which he used with his fake style and flamboyance. In short, all the fakeness that I needed and all the things that Arjun did without any effort. But it was only now that I noticed and appreciated them. By the end of the ceremony we had exchanged numbers and promised to meet the very next day.

Within a week we were talking endless hours on phone, online and through messages. I even told Arjun about him when we had our online chat at night. I wanted to know his reaction, wanted the assurance that he would be hurt and he was. He listened patiently to my blabbering about the great guy I met and then signed off without the usual "take care".

That's all I needed, to not take care.

I knew what I was doing was rash and ridiculous. Mudit was the kind of person I could never get attracted to. The only surety I needed was that he should not. Of all my kinks, I did not want to end up using someone. But his actions were enough to make me realize that he was just the kind of person I could befriend. Within a short span, we crossed all lines of what could be defined as normal modes of behavior termed appropriate for just friends. I did not know what kind of vibes I sent out to him, but whatever they were, they were enough for him to make progress. I wasn't complaining. I knew that the next time I would face Arjun; my eyes would say it all and make him move on.

A week of our acquaintance and I had achieved what I had set out to achieve.

Enough that I asked Mudit to stop.

Enough to hurt Arjun; in short just enough. I had won.

Arjun called me when I was with Mudit and I picked up, just to prove that I had moved on. The voice that I heard on the other end of the phone was amused, he was laughing at me, I didn't mind. He just told me that he would land the next day and would expect me at the airport and again without saying the usual "take care", he was gone.

"Who was it?" Mudit asked and I lied. Telling him about Arjun would have included letting him in to my world and it was mine where no one was allowed. I had an ironically superficial relationship with Mudit. We never had long personal talks; never shared the little anecdotes that help a new relationship flourish. I wanted to keep it that way because very soon, as soon as Arjun gave up on me I was planning to give up on Mudit. It was simpler to not talk about personal details. The advantage with Mudit was that he never even persisted. Sometimes I felt that we shared the same sentiment for each other, convenience.

In the sanity of the day, my guilt arose, not because I regretted it but because I felt really bad for Mudit. I had used him. I had lied to him. He had asked me if I was single and I had replied in affirmative, which was true physically but emotionally no, I wasn't. My hand was still intertwined in the pinkish hand at the airport parking. If I closed my eyes, I could still see the shape of each finger, each knuckle as those fingers closed over mine. I could feel the touch of Arjun's hand over mine. On the other hand, I never felt anything when I was with Mudit. I could not even remember the shape of his hand. And I felt bad, real bad. If I could just confess to him about it, just tell him that I am not attracted to him and can never be because I already am subdued by someone far beyond my league. I lacked the courage to do that and so in the hours that followed I was slowly poisoned by those thoughts.

Next day I took an off from work and was standing at the airport to receive Arjun. My head held high, I knew he would give up on me finally and I would be free.

Arjun walked in moments later with a blonde girl in tow whom he introduced as his colleague from work. She was sweet and smiled a lot, with her every flash of teeth I had a strong urge to break them all. Throughout the drive from the airport to my house, Arjun kept whispering something in her ear and she kept smiling. They held hands and I kept looking out of the window. He had indeed given up on me, but I failed to feel the right kind of happiness at my victory.

Hours after his arrival, Arjun knocked at my door.

"So, now I am real enough for you?"

I did not get his question. So I refused to answer him. He kept looking at me and his eyes were difficult to read, it was not anger, it was not resentment, it was something which I had never seen before. We stood like that for few seconds and then I broke down.

"Why did you make me do this, Resha?" he asked and I had no answer. I had no answer for my suspicion, for my inability to believe. That question was enough for me to jolt back to reality though.

"You go back Arjun, you don't belong here."

"That's for me to decide."

"And me as well" I added.

"And where do you think you belong?" he questioned.

The only answer I had was "nowhere" but that was not acceptable.

I had a kink.

"Can you not get really infuriated and leave?" I asked him instead.

"No I would just find a way to get back to you and we can play at this forever and play at other people too, what say?"

He never once asked me why I so wanted him to leave, I won't have been able to answer if he would have asked me anyway. I was a hypocrite, I missed him terribly when he left and showed that I didn't give a damn when he arrived. I was scared, scared of revealing my true self, scared of showing him how much he really mattered to me. But he knew and that's why he understood and that's why he forgave.

(iv)

Arjun continued his very obvious PDA in my house and I was subjected to disapproving looks from my parents because my loss was that blonde's gain. All of which made me see Mudit yet again, the idea was to be honest with him, tell him that I was still haunted by the ghosts from the past; the giant, very handsome ghost actively showcasing his talents in my drawing room right now was enough to make me run to the fake mirage. I decided to drop in enough hints to make him understand my viewpoint.

Make me less of a sinner.

"So Mudit would you be concerned if your girlfriend had had past relationships?" I asked him just for the sake of conversation.

He looked unperturbed and continued typing on his computer without as much as battling an eyelid, even as he replied in negative and then added a question of his own.

"Are you suggesting that you're my girlfriend?"

Good question. Nothing was official between us. We were just hanging out, not officially dating each other, not officially declared a couple and not officially bound to be together, so how did this thing work?

In our favour.

For now.

"No I'm not, it was a hypothetical question."

He nodded.

"Would you be concerned if I had a past?"

"I guess no."

He did not answer my question; I ended up answering my own question.

He kept looking at me for some time and then raised his hand to touch the dark circles under my eyes.

"Losing your sleep over something honey?" I winced at the endearment but did not reply.

"Some past haunting you?"

I chickened out.

"Will you fall into a relationship just to get out of an old one?" I asked instead.

Mudit smiled, maybe he got my hints.

"No, I won't. I would wait until the wounds healed." He replied with all the sincerity.

"I would." I nearly whispered.

"You would, what?"

"Fall into a relationship on rebound." I looked straight at him.

"I still won't." He smiled. He thought my confession was to trap him. My confession was the truth which bypassed his egotistical mind.

I could not bring myself to be upfront about it to him and with the passage of time and the deepening of Arjun's affection for the blonde my dark circles deepened. Mudit was a mute spectator and I felt like I was cheating him, I did not have the courage to call it off. I made sure that I meet him everyday. It gave me something else to do, even when my mind was preoccupied, it was a nice escape. I enjoyed the attention, wanted someone, something to fall back to, show off to.

Whenever I stepped out of the house, Arjun would give me a knowing smile like we were sharing a secret.

"I'm going out" I would yell out to no one in particular, just so that Arjun could hear and know whom I was going to be with. He kept smiling with no remorse and no regrets.

He confronted me on the last day of his visit as I was stepping out of the house.

"I got your point, you need not do this anymore." He said as I looked at him and feigned ignorance.

"I'm getting married." He announced.

This time I smiled and walked out of the house.

It's true in a way, when the door to your heart is tight shut, nothing can penetrate it, and you just feel an occasional tug, when your deep asleep morals sometimes wake up to give you sleepless nights instead. I still was having the fling with Mudit; my mind would be miles away when Mudit's brain concentrated on me which was not fair to anyone. But it wasn't like I was addicted. He wasn't even my antidote on the addiction to Arjun. It was just a bad case of drug overdose, where you take one medicine and it overreacts and then you are given another one and the side effects are even bad. I was suffering from many of the effects. I did not even know where I would land at the end of it all, maybe in a mental asylum, but I was ready to take any bet to not land up being with Arjun. I surely had a kink.

The week was up and it was time for Arjun to go back and needless to add time for me to say bye to Mudit, but even that was difficult. I could not. I had something very human left in me. I could not do this either, he made it easier on me though. He just vanished. I would be a hypocrite if I declare that I was happy about it. I was sad and hurt, deeply hurt. My ego was battered, I felt used and thrown. My mind went over a thousand reasons over why he would do it to me. No email, no phone call, no text message, nothing. When earlier I was bombarded with obscenely high amount of his presence, his absence was hurting. He just vanished in thin air. Like he never even existed, did I deserve this treatment? Looking at my intentions in the first place maybe I did. Does anyone deserve this treatment? Answer to this is simple. A simple, plain No.

It was the age old hunter became the hunted syndrome.

Would it make a difference to Mudit if he somehow knew all this?

If I had confessed my intentions earlier?

I figured out that it won't make a difference to him, that he had achieved all that he set out to achieve for himself and somewhere in some part of the world he was beaming to himself. I felt a bit happy for him and a hell lot sad for me when I knew I had no right to.

And somehow I also set upon thinking many other things, the simplicity of age old rules, how straightforward and easy to follow they were. How important it is for things to be official. When one can demand, complaint and if need arise legalize, would have I done that? Somehow in the modernization I had accepted myself as an independent being where the answers to questions like, "where are we going?", "Does this have a future?" did not matter. I was the kind of person who did not believe in forever. So I had no right to complain. I deserved being deserted; I can't even call it being that, it would be too brazen. I deserved every bit of it, but I could not silence my heart which kept screaming foul, only because it wanted to hold back. It was used to the attention, the endearments. It's silly how when one gets used to the fakeness, the hardheartedness, the things our elders turn their noses at and we youngsters flaunt on the roads so shamelessly, it's difficult to turn back.

It's like smoking, everyone knows it's bad, but no one gives up.

Mudit was smoking for me I wasn't ready to give up.

Arjun was the Alcohol anonymous, I wasn't even ready to enrol; someone had to make me forcefully join it.

I wasn't a feminist demanding my set of rights. I was just laughing over the irony of the situation as I drove Arjun back to the airport the next day.

Me, a single girl, who did not believe in forever, who did not believe in the too real Arjun sitting comfortably in the back seat with the blonde, his hand resting comfortably on her leg and both of them deep in conversation. He was still shy, talked very little, but she made up with her dazzling smile.

They belonged together and I belonged in my own schizoid world. I would have been thrilled if things would have worked between Mudit and me the way they worked for Arjun and the blonde. We indeed were like-minded, of the same league, no one gave us a second look when we walked together, while with Arjun people always looked, they wanted to know what a simple girl next door was doing with someone so statuesque like Arjun and he worsened it when he spoke, when he put the weight of his brooding eyes on someone as he argued with his flawless logic. People looked up to him and they looked down upon me. I wasn't ready to go down and Mudit had helped to get my bearings, see the good in me. But that's the whole irony of playing games with people; one does not always end on the winning side.

Whatever I had with Mudit defied any rational explanation.

I had concentrated on my moment with Arjun when I would explain him all in excruciating detail so as to make him hate me. But I was denied that pleasure too, he never asked me, he somehow had drawn his own conclusions in that one phone call and in reply had thrown the blonde at me.

Some years later, my friend asked me why I needed Mudit to let go of Arjun, considering the fact that Arjun had not even let go of me, he had just played my game at me.

But the fact was the blonde never let go of him.

"What about you?" she asked me next.

Why won't I give it a try?

What was I so scared of that I could not give Arjun a chance?

I had all the answers neatly stacked in my brain, but they were inexplicable.

"What about you now?" she asked me again.

"But it never was for my sake." I replied.

Epilogue

If this was a novel, I would end it with the final word describing the current location of every character. I never thought of it, while writing the stories. I was a spectator who documented a brief event before her and then the characters moved on with their lives and I moved to the next story.

As an afterthought, I can imagine where all of them landed. They all were born under my imagination and as the words appeared on paper, the essence of the characters, their souls floated away from me. Now I find them on the streets of Pune or Mumbai when I go there. I met Ananya and Shreya once when I was dining out, they got back together and from the look of it, they were happy to find solace in each other. On another occasion, I ran into Mr. Seth, he was walking hand in hand with his grand-daughter with a complacent smile upon his lips.

I stopped for a cup of coffee on the Mumbai-Pune expressway and I saw the car of the girl who went there from "the highway". She was deep in conversation with her friend, so I left her alone. I don't think she would have been happy to acknowledge my presence in front of her friend. Anyway she was too spellbound to have noticed me.

Some of them are polite enough to come back to me and say a hello, while others have moved on with their lives. On a recent visit to Goa, I had the company of Brendan walking on the beaches while Trisha chose to ignore me.

Such is life, I cannot claim anyone even if I made them, it's like the Achilles' Heel, I still have not found theirs, but they have found mine, I am in love with them and they just have to call me to make me go back to sorting their complicated lives for them, to make their lives perfect. They would find me walking the bylanes of Shimla, trying to make my life ideal.

Like Shraddha said, "*The final destination is perfection but we need to learn a lot before we reach there.*"

Them and I, we got a lot of learning to do before we claim perfection.

Acknowledgements

This book would not be complete without the support of some people who need a mention here.

Foremost, I am thankful to my mother for her endless support. Over the years she had been the mother-ship who was lenient enough to let me wander. Without her, I would not have dared to write a single word.

My friends — Sonali and Ragini — for enduring my frequent mood swings and providing honest feedback on every thing I wrote. Most of the stories included here are a result of the endless chats that we three had at evenings.

My sisters for keeping me rooted.

Lastly, I am thankful to Prashanta and everyone at Global Vision Press for their encouraging words. They were patient enough to re-read all the rough forms of draft I provided and helped me refine it into a presentable book. They were also very tolerant towards my frequent mind changes.